Walkers ON THE Run

OLDSTERS *Love* ADVENTURES
BOOK 1

C. S. KJAR

THE LAVENDER PEN

C. S. KJAR
OWNER/AUTHOR
cskjar.com

THE LAVENDER PEN
C.S. KJAR
OWNER/AUTHOR
cskjar.com

DEDICATION

This book is dedicated to everyone who has lived at least five decades. May future decades bring you laughter, fun, and good health.

FOREWORD

In 2016, I released a book called *Blessings From the Wrong Side of Town*. It never did very well even though it received good reviews. Even after ads and pushing the book on various platforms, it fizzled. The book settled to the bottom of every list.

I loved the characters too much to let them fade into memory, so I performed CPR (copy, paste, rewrite) and revived them. This book, *Walkers on the Run*, is a reimagined and rewritten version of that book. The characters are a little younger and a new character in the form of Prissy the cat joins the cast. Their story will not stop after the initial mystery, but Leona, Betty, and Clarence will continue to find more trouble in additional books. Yes, my friends, *Walkers on the Run* is Book One of the Oldsters Love Adventures series. You are never too old to enjoy life.

Walkers ON THE Run

CHAPTER 1

Leona Walker didn't think the day could get worse, but she was wrong. Attending the funeral of Al Watson, a high school classmate, was bad enough. Listening to her older sister Betty Drummond bicker with their neighbor Clarence Brown about what it felt like to die made her insides feel like they were collapsing like a star about to go supernova.

Leona pulled her minivan into the garage beside her late husband Joe's treasured 1967 Cadillac Eldorado, a giant car that took up most of the room. She wanted to get rid of it, but Joe would turn in his grave if she did. To preserve his resting in peace, she left the car as it was.

The three of them made their way to the back of the minivan where the back hatch was open. Betty helped Clarence get his walker out, then reached for her cane. Ten years earlier, the drunk driver that hit Clarence's car had left him lame and his wife dead. He wasn't ambulatory without the extra support provided by the wheeled aid.

Leona put a small package of ham and a tub of potato salad on the seat of his walker. "There's your supper."

1

He thanked her for the ride and started down the driveway toward his house across the street. The walker's wheel let out a squeal with each turn. With all the mileage Clarence had put on it, the contraption was due for a lube job.

"Clarence! Oil that wheel!" She handed Betty large bowls of cole slaw and jello salad. "It sounds like a back-up alarm."

He waved his hand in the air as if he heard, but Leona knew the sound was likely too high pitched to get picked up by his hearing aids. If he couldn't hear it, it did not exist and consequently, the wheel was never oiled and never would be. All the neighbors along the older, tree-lined street in Red Creek, South Dakota knew who was outside when the squeal sounded. Everyone in the state probably heard it.

After the funeral for Al Watson, she and the rest of the Christian church group served lunch to the family and cleaned up, and as usual, made too much. Afterward, they'd all divided the leftovers to take home. With stacked food containers in one arm and her keys in the other hand, she was anxious to rest for a while after an emotional morning. Her feet, back, and head hurt. She'd send Betty off to her room and relax in her recliner with Hallmark channel lulling her to sleep.

She unlocked the garage door that led into her kitchen and pushed the door open with her foot. Betty's cat Prissy shot out the door like a yellow-and-white cannonball, almost knocking Leona off balance. Prissy ricocheted off the minivan and flew past Betty who had an armful of leftovers. The cat's trajectory startled Betty, and plastic food storage containers went flying in every direction.

Betty followed her cat, hustling after her as fast as her 74-year-old legs and her cane would carry her. "Prissy! What's wrong? Prissy, come back!"

Leona stared at the mess on her garage floor. Several of the containers had busted open, their contents splattered in a starburst pattern across the side of the van, the walls, and the floor. A glob of jello salad crawled down the wall like a creature searching for its habitat.

A screech tumbled from Leona's mouth. "Betty, your dumb cat made this mess. You're cleaning it up!"

Ready to go sit in her recliner, she turned back to the opened door. Her mouth went dry, and her arms lost their strength. She stepped slowly into her kitchen. A glance around sent an Arctic wind through her veins. She blinked her eyes several times trying to refocus, hoping that she wasn't really seeing what she was seeing. The view didn't change.

Broken china, shattered coffee cups, and silverware were strewn all over the floor. The contents of their cabinets and pantry had been opened and emptied across the debris. The vandals had hurled the tin and glass containers against the wall where they left their mark on impact. Flour, sugar, and spices covered everything in the kitchen. The refrigerator door stood open. Everything had been emptied except for the vegetable drawer. Ketchup and mustard slowly oozed down the kitchen walls and stained both the floor and countertops. Broken eggs were everywhere. Food-covered footprints tracked into the living room.

She let out a cry. "Oh. My. STARS!" She hesitated before taking another step, looking for clues and listening for sounds. Anything that would tell her why the hair on the back of her neck was standing up.

Betty's footsteps and panting came from the garage. "What's wrong, Prissy? Settle down." Betty crooned to her meowing pet in her arms. "Were you that lonely?" Prissy hissed. "Oh, you silly cat. What's gotten into you?"

Betty came up behind Leona and gasped. "I did NOT make this mess. I'm not cleaning it."

Leona set her food containers on the syrup-covered countertop. She held her purse close to make sure it wouldn't touch the sticky mess. "I know you didn't, but who did?"

The two women crept into the living room. The room was in total disarray, with everything upended or on its side. The furniture upholstery was shredded like someone with a chainsaw came through. In the middle of the floor, their gallon of milk and a bottle of bleach were overturned and surrounded by wet carpet. The stench of bleach filled the air.

Leona put her hand over her nose and mouth and pushed Betty back into the most undisturbed corner of the kitchen. She held her hand over her heart to keep it steady and tried to regain her composure. "I'll go check the other rooms," she whispered. She scanned the floor for a safe place to step.

"No!" Betty held onto her clothes with one hand and held Prissy with the other. "Someone might still be in here! Let's go to Clarence's house and call the police from there." She tugged on

Leona's arm until she followed her out of the garage. They hurried across the street.

Clarence had just unlocked his front door when the two women yelled out to him in unison. "Our house has been robbed!"

Leona cried out. "Everything is in ruins!"

Clarence's mouth fell open. "What? Are you sure?"

Leona stopped at the edge of the ramp that led to his front porch and leaned on the railing to catch her breath. "Am I sure? Trust me! I didn't leave my house that way! Oh, my word! It's awful!" She wiped the tears from her face before she put her arm around Betty and Prissy and led them to his front door. "We have to call the police."

Clarence stood wide-eyed in his doorway, glancing first at the two distraught women, then to the house across the street, and back again. "Come in and sit down." He motioned them inside, then shuffled over to the sofa, and moved a pile of newspapers onto the coffee table.

"Clarence, call the police for me." Leona dried her eyes a little. "I'm too upset to do it." She sat on one end of the sofa and let Betty and Prissy have the other.

Clarence fumbled with his pocket and found his phone. He flipped his tiny device open. "Now, let's see. That's nine..." He pushed a button. "Oops. That's nine..." He pushed again. "One." He pushed another button. "Oops. Why do they make buttons so small when I have such big fingers?"

"Never mind!" Leona got her phone out of her purse and dialed 911. "Send the police. I've been robbed! Come quick!"

5

"From where are you calling?"

"I'm calling from 6315 South Harwood Circle. Someone has gone through my house and destroyed it."

"Are you in danger?"

"No, but I catch who did this, they are for sure."

"Is anything missing?"

She paused for a moment. "I don't know if they took anything. I couldn't see past the mess they made to know what's there and what's missing. I was afraid to go look because the thieves might still be in there, and so I'm at the neighbor's house and—and—they might have guns and knives. Come quickly!"

CHAPTER 2

"Wipe your feet before you go in," Leona cried out. She stood in her garage behind Police Officer Don Janus and his young partner, Olivia Torrez, as they started to enter the kitchen. Her habitual words spilled out without her permission. She knew they made no sense. Her brain was so overloaded she couldn't think straight.

Olivia turned to look at her and put her hand on Leona's shoulder. "I don't think it'll make much difference."

Leona covered her face with her hands. "Of course, it won't. I'm sorry."

She felt Olivia give her a soft pat. "Why don't you go sit on the front porch while we have a look around. We'll come out there and let you know what we find."

"Lord, give me strength," Leona whispered as she heard crunching footsteps in her ruined kitchen. As she turned to go, she heard them talking.

"Wow, they really did a number on this place, didn't they? None of the others was this bad." Don turned to Olivia. "Did you put in a call for Detective Smythe?"

"Yes, before we got out of the car."

7

With a final glance at the spilled food on her garage floor and wall and the side of her minivan, she made her way to the large, covered porch that ran the length of the house's front. At least they hadn't ruined anything outside her house. Her flower beds and neatly mowed lawn looked the same. She'd always been proud of how nice she and Joe kept their yard. It was slightly better than the neighbors, except for the city councilman who lived at the end of the block. His exceptional gardens and lawn were seen after by a landscape company, which was like cheating when everyone else did their own.

Her padded rocking chair's embrace welcomed and comforted her. She rubbed her temples trying to relieve the stress. Why did Joe have to die two years ago? He should be here to help. He'd always handled these kinds of things. She ground her teeth. They were supposed to spend a long retirement together, but he got sick and died shortly after. It was unfair! How was she supposed to put their home back together by herself?

A squeaking wheel drifted to her ear. Looking up, Leona saw Betty and Clarence coming up the driveway. Still carrying Prissy, Betty rushed up the porch ramp that Joe had built after Clarence had his installed. Leona caught her arm before she could go into the house. "Stay out here with me. I can't look at it again."

Betty stopped in her tracks and whimpered as she rubbed Prissy's back. "I was afraid of that. What will we do? Where will we go?" She held her cat up to her cheeks. "My precious Prissy, no wonder you were terrified. You witnessed horrible things. I'm so thankful you're safe." Her voice broke as she snuggled her face into the fur.

Catching Betty's cane before it fell to the ground, Leona was thankful she didn't have to bend down to pick it up. She guided Betty to Joe's chair beside her. Clarence sat in his usual chair on the other side of Betty and parked his walker, clanging and banging it as he did so.

Questions floated in Leona's head. Who would do this? What was taken? Where would they stay? What next? Answers flitted around like fireflies, disappearing as she got closer to them, leaving her with nothing to grasp.

"I called our coffee group," Clarence squeezed Betty's outstretched hand. "They should be here soon."

Leona groaned. "Not now, Clarence," she uttered through her clinched teeth. "I don't want to deal with them before I know how bad things are. Carly will come in here and tell me all the things I did wrong and what I need to do now and on and on. I can't handle that know-it-all and her incessant talking right now. I've got enough junk to deal with."

Clarence cleared his throat as he usually did when he was about to lecture someone. He looked Leona square in the face. "You need support in this crisis, and they want to help. They're your friends. George said he'd call his son since he knows you have homeowner's insurance with him. He'll probably come, too." He turned back to sit straight in his chair. "That's one less thing you have to worry about."

Betty set Prissy in her lap where the cat curled into a ball. "Speaking of calling his son, we should call our kids. They might come help clean the house."

Leona raised her face to the heavens and sent a prayer for strength. She'd rather face Carly than her kids. Since Joe died, Jennifer and Brett had given unwanted advice at every turn, like she was suddenly incapable of taking care of herself. It felt like they conspired on what she should do now that their dad was gone because they were usually united in their opinions. They urged her to sell the house and move closer to one of them, but she couldn't. She and Joe had built this house to raise their kids and grow old in. At 68, she wasn't old yet.

She and her kids argued when Leona took Betty in after she had a stroke that left her weakened. Her daughter Diane wanted to put her in assisted living, but Betty's finances weren't enough to handle it. Diane owned a business and didn't have time to take care of her mother, but Leona did. It filled a void after losing Joe.

A car drove down the street and pulled into the driveway of the house at the end of the block, bringing Leona back to the present. Betty cooed to Prissy, and Clarence's head tilted forward against his chest as he softly snored. Other than the police car out front and neighbors peeking through their windows wondering what was happening at her house, things were normal for a Saturday afternoon.

Leona was thankful for the moment of peace. Her coffee group would soon come and crowd around her when what she wanted most was to boot everyone out so she could sit in the rubble of her home with a bottle of glue, a wet rag, and a bucket of Chlorox water. She could start to piece her things, her treasures, and her sense of normalcy back into place.

George and Irene Donovan were the first to arrive, bringing an unexpected smile to Leona's face. She loved Irene who would help fend off Carly's barbs.

George waved as they got out of Irene's car. His heart was as large as his massive frame that had served him well during college football, but now was a detriment to his arthritis-plagued joints. Irene was always nicely dressed, with her graying hair elegantly styled to complement her short, chunky, grandmotherly size. Her heart was as big as her husband's.

George told Leona not to get up. He gave her shoulder a firm squeeze before going to hug Betty as she moved to the porch swing. After shaking Clarence's hand, he went into the house to look around.

"We called George Junior," Irene bent to hug Leona, then sat in Joe's chair. "He's on his way now. He said to tell you not to worry, your insurance policy will take care of everything."

"I hadn't even thought that far ahead."

Someone started opening windows behind them. George walked out of the house shaking his head and coughing. "Wow, they made a mess in there. If it were a car, I'd declare it totaled." Irene started to go in, but he held her back. "Stay with the ladies, please." He walked to the end of the driveway and waved as George Junior pulled up in his large SUV. They talked together as they walked up the ramp. George Junior had taken over his father's insurance business, so they spoke the same business language.

George Junior knelt in front of Leona. He was as large as his father, and she had to look up. "Mrs. Walker, don't worry about this. You're covered. You can stay at a hotel until we get your house back into shape. I'll take some photos to document the damage and get the paperwork started." He stood up, his knees popping as he did. "We'll need a list of the items that were destroyed so we can submit it for reimbursement. Can you do that?"

"Of course, I can." A flash of heat ran through her core. Why did people have to keep implying she couldn't do things? She was perfectly capable of doing anything they could do. Her ire was tinted with a shade of guilt. Both generations of Donovans were trying to help. No need to get snippy about it. "It may take a while. It's hard to know what's missing until I clean up the mess."

"You don't have to do it today. Just sometime in the next week. Our policies require that we send a list in." George Junior and George Senior murmured soft words of encouragement to Leona before they went into the house.

Leona nodded, not knowing what else to do. She looked up as a black car parked at the curb in front of Clarence's house. A tall, lean man got out and quickly surveyed the scene and surrounding area. Dark hair, dark suit, and dark glasses, he marched toward them like a man in command of everything.

Leona sat up straighter in her chair. Maybe this was the head police guy, the one most efficient at solving crimes. He'd track down the scoundrels in no time. She couldn't stop the smile that spread across her face. Hope at last!

"I got here as soon as I could," he announced like he was Joe Friday.

Before Leona could respond, the voice of Don Janus came from behind her. "Thanks for coming. Detective Bradley Smythe, this is Leona Walker, the owner of the home."

The man looked in her direction as he marched up the ramp. He shook her hand firmly. "Call me Smythe." He turned toward Don behind him. "Show me what you got." The two men went into the house.

Betty rocked herself on the porch swing. "He's not overly friendly, is he?"

"He's obviously a busy man," Leona told her friends as she rubbed her fingers to restore their warmth. "His hands were like ice. Maybe he has a warm heart. I hope he wastes no time solving this crime."

George Sr. sat in a sturdy chair alongside Clarence. "They say the police are very busy these days. Still, police need to have good bedside manners like doctors. Why, in the old days—"

A white Cadillac Escalade pulled up in front of the house. Before the motor was turned off, Carly Sophris got out in regal form. Being the wife of a bank president had given her an overabundance of self-importance. Dressed in black leggings and a red sparkly tunic, her dark hair and her overdone makeup made her look like she was trying way too hard to appear young.

Carly strutted up the ramp to the front porch like a peacock looking to impress anyone in the vicinity. Leona didn't get out of her chair as Carly tried to hug her. She had to hold her breath, so she didn't choke on the thick scent of perfume.

"Leona, darling. I'm sorry you're going through all this. If you had a burglar alarm, it might not have happened. Smart people have burglar alarms on their houses. Or a gun." She made her way to the other end of the porch in her high heeled sandals.

"A gun?" Leona pulled back. What was this crazy woman talking about? "I don't own a gun because I couldn't shoot anybody."

Carly's eyebrows tried to reach her hairline. "No gun? I thought all Texas women owned a gun." She clicked her tongue.

"I haven't lived in Texas for 50 years. I'm more South Dakotan than Texan."

"You can't tell it by the way you drawl when you talk." Carly let out a little giggle. "You really need to get rid of that accent if you're going to call yourself a native of this state, dear."

Carly's long-suffering husband, Nick, walked onto the porch and shook everyone's hand. "Don't mind her. She's just running her mouth off," he said so low only Leona could hear it. A tall and distinguished-looking man, his kind manners and patient wisdom were eclipsed by his wife's overpowering presence. Leona admired him as much as she pitied him being married to such an obnoxious person.

Carly ceremoniously leaned against the porch railing. "It's a good thing you were at Al Watson's funeral when this happened. Otherwise, you might have been murdered."

Her statement sucked any sort of amiability from the air. Everyone acted like they'd been turned to stone. Except for Betty. She got hysterical with howling and pulling at her hair. Leona got up and tried to calm her, but she'd have none of it.

"If our friend Al hadn't died, we'd be dead," Betty cried out. "Don't you know what this means? Al Watson saved us by dying!" She broke down in sobs. "That—that dear man! We owe him our lives!"

Only flies and Betty moved under the covered porch. Everyone else remained still and silent with gaping mouths until Leona cried out above Betty's weeping. "That's preposterous, Betty. Al didn't die because of us. He smoked, was obese, and had bad kidneys. It was a coincidence. Get a hold of yourself!"

"I don't care what you say. I think Al is our hero." Betty pulled a tissue out of her purse and wiped her nose. "He saved us from being killed." She cried into the tissue.

Carly's eyes rolled and blinked. "You're nuts! Maybe you two should move into an independent living facility. People can keep an eye on you there."

"That's enough of that, Carly." Nick stepped between her and the rest of the group.

"But, darling, this certainly wouldn't have happened if they'd been someplace where criminals couldn't break in, like a gated community where we live. This part of town is so old, and it naturally draws the scum of society. They really should think about moving..."

"Dear, this is one of the nicest and oldest parts of town. It's prime real estate."

Their bickering was driving Leona mad. "Thank you, Nick. The only problem with this neighborhood is most people work during the day, so no one is left to watch what goes on except me. And when I'm gone, see what happens?" She waved her hands toward her front door.

Smythe came out on the porch, closely followed by the two police officers, George Junior, and the smell of bleach. Carly switched topics and continued to prattle about how overworked and underpaid law enforcement was. Her voice went up an octave as she babbled on about how much she supported them.

She didn't quit prattling until Smythe did something no one else had ever been able to do. He held up his hand to Carly and she quit talking. Leona was amazed. Whatever power he had, she wanted it too.

Turning to face Leona, Smythe stood with his feet wide. "Worst burglary I've seen yet. We've had a rash of them across town, but none of the others had damage as bad as this."

"But why me? What did I do to them?"

His eyes scanned the ceiling of her porch like he was looking for clues. "Maybe they were having a bad day and took it out on you."

Carly moved to stand beside the detective, mirroring his posture. "You know what I think? I think they were just having a good time. They loved being in a house without a security system. Don't you?"

The detective's jaw went slack but otherwise he didn't flinch. "I don't know. I'll ask them when we catch them." He turned away from Carly and continued. "I'll need the same list you provide to the insurance company so we can watch for your possessions. If you have photos of any of the missing items, they would be very helpful."

Staring into his dark glasses, Leona nodded. Her stomach knotted a little, thinking about the enormous chore in front of her. "I'll get it done as soon as possible."

"My department will be in touch if we find anything." He reached inside his suit pocket and pulled out a little wallet. Taking out his business card, he handed it to Leona. "We appreciate your cooperation." With that, he turned on his heel and left them all looking after him as he walked to his car.

Olivia gave Leona her business card too. "Call me when you have a list of the missing items, and I'll come pick it up if you like. Or call me if you have any questions. Keep your doors locked at all times. If you see something or someone suspicious, call us at once." She paused a second or two. "I'm sorry for your losses." Don and Olivia left right behind the detective.

Leona stared at the business cards in her hand. She'd never forgive Joe for leaving her alone to deal with this mess. They should be sitting on the beach in Hawaii, drinking pineapple drinks and watching the sunset into the ocean. Instead, she was left to put her house back in order by herself. Her eyes burned.

George Junior waved his phone at Leona, pulling her out of her thoughts. "I'll take a few more photos and start your claim as soon as I get back to the office. I'll make reservations for you and Betty at the Extended Stay Hotel and have them send the bill to me." He disappeared back into the house.

George Senior leaned on the porch rail. "Don't clean this up yourself. Buy some new clothes, enough to last a few days, and spend the rest of today at the hotel. After a day of serving food and cleaning up the church kitchen, you need the rest, plus the fumes are too bad for anyone to be in there. Leave the windows open so it can air out. Junior will send a cleaning crew tomorrow or the next day to work on it. Trust me, everything will be back to the way it was before you know it."

Leona gave the man a hug. "Thanks, George. I want to go through the—the debris and salvage what I can. Plus, I can start that list."

"Give it a couple of days. The bleach fumes are strong enough to make your eyes and throat burn if you're in it too long. The cleaning crew will rip out the carpet which will help. Let the vapors dissipate before coming back."

Betty walked up beside Leona. "I want to go through my room, too. I had so many mementos in there. I don't know what I'll do if they're all gone." She teared up a little, and George gave her a hug.

"I hope you find them after the house is aired out. Work with the crew. They'll help you sort through everything and figure out what can be fixed and what should be thrown away."

18

Carly pushed her way through people to stand in front of Leona. "You can bet those people who clean up this place will pocket anything of value they find. You better be here the whole time, watching them like hawks. Otherwise, they'll steal you blind." She crossed her arms and lifted her brows as high as they could go as she tilted her head.

Nick stepped beside his wife and took her by the elbow. "Time to go, Carly." He pulled her along with him, her heels clanking on the ramp. "Talk to you tomorrow, everyone," He kept going as Carly sputtered along beside him.

"Nick, these poor women need our help! We can't go now!" She pulled her arm back, but Nick grabbed it again. She turned to look back at the front porch. "Leona. Betty. Let us know if we can help you arrange your new furniture. We are available to you at any time." Nick tugged harder on Carly until she followed.

The others stood in silence until the large SUV pulled away. The birds in the nearby tree broke out a cheerful song, as if they were happy Carly was gone.

Betty spoke first, "Lord, forgive me for talking bad about people, but she annoys me."

Clarence cleared his throat. "She annoys everybody." He pulled his walker around to the front of the chair so it would be handy when he got up out of it. He made two attempts to get out of the low-slung wicker chair. He finally got his feet under himself and pushed his walker down the porch. "Let's have a peek inside before we go." He took a deep breath and went in.

CHAPTER 3

Leona and the others sidled into the ruined living room. Betty let out a cry of despair. Prissy squirmed free of Betty's embrace and shot out the open door.

Leona had trouble keeping her emotions under control and trying not to choke on bleach fumes. This place didn't feel like her home anymore. The serenity it once provided lay shredded and broken like all the contents.

After taking stock of the damage in the living room and kitchen, Leona crept down the hallway, peering into Betty's bedroom and the bath along the way. Betty's normally spotless room had been ransacked. Her clothes were scattered everywhere, and the drawers of her wooden chest were thrown on the bed. Betty stood in the doorway, too stunned to enter farther. Clarence remained with her as Irene and George followed Leona down the hallway to her own bedroom.

With Irene's hand on her shoulder, Leona swung her bedroom door open. Her heart nearly quit beating, her body trembled, and her throat constricted. The bureau drawers had been emptied onto the bed and flung aside. She saw the edge of her jewelry box underneath clothes and unmentionables. She clawed through the pile, hoping she might find her most precious pieces left behind.

Jerking upright, she covered her mouth to keep the cry of anguish from escaping. All her jewelry was gone. The pearl necklace Joe gave her for their fortieth anniversary. The diamond bracelet for their forty-fifth anniversary only three years ago. But what hurt the most was the two things Leona most wanted to be there were gone. Her late mother's ruby necklace and Joe's wedding ring. She let out a distraught howl and began to cry. "Oh, my word! No!" she cried as she pawed through the clutter and mess on her bed.

"What is it, dear?" Irene pushed Leona's hair away from her face.

"They're gone!" Leona covered her face with her hands. "My most treasured possessions are gone!" She picked up one of her blouses off the bed and sobbed into it. Unwilling to believe it, she wiped her eyes and shuffled through the pile again, sorting clothes from underclothes as she went. She dropped to the floor and felt the carpet along the bedside and under the bed while George and Irene urged her to tell them what she was looking for.

Nothing. She sat back and clutched her aching heart. Joe's wedding ring was gone. A sob made its way past the lump in her throat and another cry of anguish escaped her lips. That ring meant more to her than anything else on earth. It was her last link to Joe.

"Are you having a heart attack?" She looked up to see Clarence leaning over his walker, peering down at her with more wrinkles than usual across his brow. He pulled his cell phone out of his pocket. "I'll call 911."

George reached out and put his hand over the phone. "No, she's not having an attack. She's grieving over what she's lost."

Betty gently nudged her sister with her cane and told her to get up off the floor and sit on the bed. "Did they get Momma's necklace?"

Leona nodded without looking at her.

"Oh no! Not Momma's ruby necklace!" Betty sat beside her sister and sobbed along with her.

When the crying subsided, Leona wiped her eyes with her hands. Irene got toilet paper out of the bathroom. She handed some to both of them but kept a small piece to wipe her own eyes.

The toilet tissue was black when Leona looked at it. Embarrassed for her friends to see her like that, Leona hurried into the master bath and looked in the mirror. Her mascara had run down her face and turned her normally pleasant expression into something from a zombie movie. One rub of a moistened face wipe, and she looked better. Less zombie like.

Irene stood in the doorway, her eyes red around the bottom. "What can I do for you, Leona?"

Leona shook her head, then wiped her face again. "Nothing. It's gone, and I have to accept it." The breath she drew in was ragged. "I'm over the shock and ready to get to work." It was a lie, but she didn't want her friends to fuss over her.

Irene guided her through the kitchen and out the front door to the porch where the air was fresh and clean. George led Clarence and Betty out behind them.

The sunshine, the singing birds, and the fragrance of flowers revived Leona and reminded her the world was still turning. Most things could be replaced or restored and those that couldn't, maybe Smythe would find them. Hope still existed.

George talked about what he'd observed during his trips inside the house. Some items were unbroken, like pots, pans, and utensils, and only needed a good scrubbing to be reuseable. Not everything would need to be replaced.

Leona laughed to herself. She saw her 30-year-old Tupperware bowls had survived. Not even destructive burglars could damage Tupperware. Maybe in their rampage they'd found the two lids and one bottom that were missing before the crime.

Clarence squealed his way home and found a spiral notebook for the list George Junior and Smythe wanted. When he came back, he started listing the things the group recalled were damaged. The joint effort was a small start but having the help of her friends brought a measure of comfort.

The TV was gone. Her old turntable was gone, along with the old records she'd kept from years gone by. Her VCR player was still there but must have been used to make some of the holes in the wall. Its mangled case lay among the VHS cassettes with the tapes pulled out and tangled together. The group discussed whether to make a claim on the outdated technology. Clarence scratched it off their list, but George told him to put it back on.

The china cabinet was face down and the only unbreakable things in it were the tablecloths. Everything else was likely shattered to smithereens. Somewhere she had a photo of her grandson in front of it. If she found that photo, it would help her remember what was there.

She, Irene, Clarence, and George made progress on the list until they noticed Betty was gone. Leaving them behind to check the notes, Leona hurried inside and down the hallway to her sister's room where she found Betty picking up her clothes and hanging them up. Prissy watched from the sunny windowsill.

"Stop!" Leona cried out.

"What?" Betty stood frozen with a blouse in her hands. "I can't stand this mess! If I can get my room neatened, I would feel better."

"You're hanging up clothes that the thieves had their hands on. Goodness, sister, at least wash them before you put those filthy things back in your closet."

"On my clothes?" Betty's mouth fell open with a grimace. "Eww! I didn't think about those horrible people touching my clothes! We need to wash everything." She threw the blouse she was holding across the room and held out her hands like they had been rubbed in poison ivy.

Betty slumped onto her bed. "I don't understand who would do this. We don't have anything worth stealing. Why did they have to be so evil? I hope an elephant tramples those thieves into mud so deep they'll never see daylight again."

Fat chance of that happening, Leona thought. If and when the police found them and they came to trial, she'd be there to burn a hole through them with her laser stare. In her former life as a teacher, her students always said they could feel the burn.

25

She put an arm around her sister. "Go wash your hands, then join the rest of us."

Leona went back to the porch where the others were formulating a plan of attack for cleaning. The topic was too much to bear. Leona sat in her chair and rubbed her eyes, hoping to ease the fatigue headache that was pounding in her head. The urge to shower and go to bed was almost overwhelming, but she had nothing to put on and no place to lie down. Her head ached more.

George wrote in the spiral notebook. "I added your mother's ruby necklace to the list. In addition to those, I have the TV, the record player, and your computer and monitors. Those are the things missing. I started a second list for the things destroyed and need to be replaced, like the sofa, recliners, end tables, lamps, and china cabinet and contents. Most of your food stock has been destroyed so that goes on the list as well." George closed the spiral notebook and gave it to Leona. "It's only a start. You'll have to include your clothes, bedroom furniture, and anything else you find."

She looked through the list quickly, not really caring about it. It took considerable effort to force her brain to consider the breadth of all the damage. "I have a photo of my mother with the necklace on, but who knows where it is in this mess. I didn't take photos of my TV or things like that." Leona let out a soft laugh. "Does anyone?"

Clarence cleared his throat and readjusted his seat. "I read that you should video your house so if it gets robbed, you have documentation of your possessions. I did that quite some time ago. I probably should do it again."

George seconded the motion. "George Junior had us do it."

Leona looked across her lawn and down the street in hopes her face wouldn't show her sorrow. The whole world knew about doing this, but she'd missed the memo.

The afternoon sun was fading as evening came toward them. When darkness came, she didn't want to be in the shambles of her house. Creepy, crawly feelings squirmed up her arms. She and Betty still had to buy something to wear, go by the pharmacy to start the process of getting replacement medications, and drive to the hotel. Oh, a cat cage for Prissy. She wouldn't share a hotel room with that cat running free.

She suddenly stood up, "Let's go. We've done all we can today. I have errands to run before we can rest."

"Can I help?" Irene offered. "I could go get you new clothes and underclothes while you tend to other things. I'll bring them to you at the hotel."

And tell her what size underwear she wore? Leona would never do that. That information was as top secret as nuclear codes. It was sweet but nothing doing. Leona gave her the sweetest smile. "Thanks, but we'll pick up something."

Irene and George left to go home, promising to come back and help clean. Leona scurried off to her room to take one last look, for something, but she didn't know what. Her prescription medicines were gone, and she wouldn't wear any of these clothes ever again. She quickly turned and left.

Three days later, Leona and Betty sat in front of Smythe's cluttered desk. Several coffee mugs sat on top of a filing cabinet beside his desk, and a variety of hats, belts, and extra clothes hung from hooks on the wall. A solitary frame stood on the front edge of his desk, but Leona couldn't see the picture.

She wished she'd called Olivia Torrez instead of Smythe. She'd feel more comfortable discussing her private life with a woman than him. She didn't really know why she felt that way but couldn't deny it. Smythe seemed perfectly capable and had probably dealt with this sort of thing many times before. The awards on the wall behind him indicated he was very competent in what he did. So why did she feel uncomfortable? Maybe his aftershave didn't agree with her nose.

Smythe scanned the list that the ladies had provided, then flipped it casually onto his file-folder laden desk. He leaned back in his office chair, tapping his fingertips together. "Thanks. We'll contact all the pawnshops to keep an eye out for your jewelry. Maybe they'll turn up, but don't hold your breath. Any items with gold or silver or other valuable minerals are usually quickly sold and melted down. Pearls and diamonds are separated and used in other jewelry."

Leona's heart jumped like it had been hit with a cattle prod. She gasped while she held her chest. "Then speed is of the utmost importance. It's imperative I get my mother's ruby necklace and my husband's wedding band back. And the pearls and diamonds. Get your men on it right away!"

"Amen, sister!" Betty waved her arms. "Let's track those criminals down! Send out those APBs. Redlights. Sirens. Handcuffs. Prison!"

"Shush!" Leona squeezed Betty's forearm. She felt the same way, but decorum called for calmer methods. "Mr. Smythe, do you have a special detail looking for these criminals? I heard there has been a rash of home break-ins. Doesn't that fact point to more manpower dedicated to finding out who is doing it? Or will you only look for them during your normal activities?"

"We don't have special details for home burglaries. This is a small town with a small police force. But I assure you, we're all working on it."

"You should!" Betty called out. "This calls for immediate action. Why are you sitting around here? Let's go get 'em!" Betty rose and hustled toward the door. She stopped before leaving the room. "You coming?"

Smythe's eyebrows raised as he looked first at Leona, then scratched his nose. He waved his hand toward his piles of files on his desk. "See these? All unsolved cases. You're not the only one in town with a problem. We can't concentrate manpower on just a necklace and a ring." He paused, closed his eyes, and quickly clenched and unclenched his fists. "We'll do all we can to recover your things."

Leona leaned forward and rapped on a pile of folders. "You're telling us that we're low priority. We're taxpayers, you know. I've been paying taxes since before you were born. I think we deserve a little more consideration."

He avoided her gaze as he opened a file folder. "We'll work with the local pawnshops and keep an eye out for your things. That's the best we can do. I'll be in touch if we find out anything." He picked up a sheet of paper and studied it.

"That's not enough!" Leona stood and glared at the detective across his desk.

His droopy-eyed look of boredom transformed into a narrow-eyed stare. "The matter is under investigation. We're doing all we can." His eyes returned to the paper in front of him.

How dare he! He couldn't investigate from behind his desk! The urge to throw herself across the top of the desk and grab him by the collar swallowed her up, but a soft tug on her blouse held her back.

"Come on, Sis." Betty tugged harder. "Let him work. We told him how anxious we are to get our stuff back. We've done all we can do here. Let's go home."

Her impulses wavered between assault or backing away. Discretion won the argument. She stepped away from his desk. "I know the police chief. All his kids were in my classes. He knows who I am."

The detective slammed his hands on his desk, making the women flinch. His nostrils flared and the veins in his neck showed as he rose. Suddenly, he looked down and drew in a big breath before looking up again. His face seemed calmer. "The chief knows about the burglary. He knows we're investigating it. He knows we don't have the manpower to go door-to-door looking for your stolen necklace. He's as sorry as he can be that your house was burgled. Now, please, let me do my job." He plopped into his chair and rubbed his temples as he leaned over the paper.

Leona stomped her foot as she desperately searched for something clever or motivational to say but nothing came.

"Come on." Betty poked her sister with her cane. "We'll send out our own APBs. Thank you for your time, Mr. Smythe." She tugged on Leona who was rooted to the spot. "It's time to go home." She gave one last, harder tug, and Leona moved with her.

"We can't go home. It's smells of chlorine." Leona yelled over her shoulder as they went out the door.

"Keep your voice down." Betty steered her back to the reception area where Clarence waited for them. "Throwing a fit isn't going to make them work any harder."

"But it makes *me* feel better!" That man! Cold as the ice crystals in her old freezer that had to be defrosted every year. Didn't he understand how much Joe's ring meant to her?

Her shoulders felt like they drooped to her waist. No, she hadn't told Smythe about it. There was no way to make him understand. Without it, she didn't know if she could go on. She might die without seeing it beside her at night on Joe's pillow. That would turn this simple robbery into a murder and move her file up to the top of his unorganized heap.

Clarence stood up as he saw them approaching. "How'd it go?"

Leona growled in response and stomped her foot in frustration. "Nowhere. It went nowhere."

Betty let go of Leona and pushed Clarence's walker closer to him. "They're investigating. That's all they'll say."

"That's something. These things take time. You'll have to be patient." Clarence bumped his walker against Leona. "Don't worry. They'll find your things." He kept nudging her along toward the door.

Fed up with the prodding, Leona kicked the squeaky wheel and glared at Clarence. "They're not doing enough or going fast enough to suit me."

Betty came by her and took her by the elbow to pull her along. "Don't hurt his walker, sis. We don't want to carry him."

True, but if she broke the wheel, maybe he'd get one that didn't squeak. It was time to trade that old model in for something newer and quieter. The wheel's sound was picking at her self-control.

Clarence's walker squealed its way behind them as they slowly made their way down the sidewalk to the minivan in the handicapped space. Hopelessness filled Leona so fully that she stopped to turn around and lookback at the entry door of the police station. She was tempted to go back in and give Smythe a good lecture on what public service meant.

Clarence reached out to take Leona's arm and bring her along with him and Betty. "Leona dear, the police know what to do. Don't worry."

She jerked her arm away. "I'm not your dear! They don't care about my mother's necklace or Joe's ring. They don't understand

32

that those things are all I have left of them. All that I have to hold in my hand, knowing they touched them." Her voice broke as she despaired.

Betty put her arms around Leona's waist and squeezed. "Don't worry, Leona. I have a plan."

Leona's body stiffened as she heard the oft repeated words that usually led to trouble. Even in childhood, whenever Betty proclaimed she had a plan, it usually led straight to bed without supper. It still struck fear in her.

Betty moved Leona closer to Clarence to form a huddle. "Remember how in that TV show *Murder She Wrote*, Jessica Fletcher always takes matters into her own hands? Why don't we investigate like she did when someone was murdered? Ask a few questions and put the pieces of the puzzle together. Just like those jigsaw puzzles we work on. I bet we can solve this case."

Leona shook her head. "That's TV. This is reality. Let's go home—um, to the hotel." She pressed the buttons on her key fob and the doors on the minivan opened. As Clarence got in his seat, she folded his walker and put it in the back.

"No, really!" Betty called after her. "If the police won't do it, we can!"

Leona agreed only to settle her sister's enthusiasm and to get her in the van. Her idea would never work.

CHAPTER 4

"You missed our turn!" Betty turned in her seat as they passed through the intersection.

"We're not going home yet," Leona replied as she stopped at a red light. "I'm going to see Ernie about what I can do."

"Your lawyer?" Clarence leaned forward from the backseat. "Why him? He can't do anything for you the police and George Junior can't do."

"But what about my plan?" Betty was almost frantic. "Let's investigate for ourselves! We don't need Perry Mason to solve it for us. That would take all our fun away." She sat back in her seat, bottom lip sticking out.

When a red light brought them to a stop, Leona glanced over at her pouting sister, sitting there in her new outfit. The two of them had visited the Penney store and picked up a few nice blouses and polyester pants, plus the requisite unmentionables. New clothes had done little to assuage their grief over having to throw out their old garments, but it was better than being naked.

Leona turned back to watch the traffic light. "My house was vandalized, and I think I should see a lawyer about it. Maybe he can help get the ball rolling on the investigation. He could threaten to

35

file a lawsuit. Maybe that would put a fire under Smythe's chair." She could feel her anger rising. "The police should have kept us safe from those hoodlums! As it happened, I'm glad we were at Al's funeral instead of at home."

Betty cried out, "That dear sweet man!" Her eyes full of tears, she grabbed Leona by the upper arm. "How can we ever repay him for saving our lives?" She covered her face with her hands and let out a sob. "What a wonderful man! He saved us from being murdered!" She howled more as she dug in her purse for tissues.

Not this ludicrous idea again.

"That's ridiculous!" Clarence reached past the seat back to pat Betty's shoulders. "We wouldn't have been murdered. Burglars don't come if you're home. Dry your tears. There's no reason to cry." He leaned forward and poked Leona's shoulder. "You're her sister. Tell her it's okay."

"Hush now, Betty." Leona reached over to pat her arm. "Thieves don't kill people. They take what's not theirs."

"But it could be true. We might have been killed for our clothes and TV set if we'd been home. Oh sweet, sweet Al. He'll always be my hero!" She wiped her eyes.

Leona looked toward heaven and sent up a prayer for help. In doing so, she missed the light turning green. The car behind them tapped the horn, signaling that her prayer had taken too long. The universe was nagging her. She frowned in the rearview mirror and drove on as Betty sniffled.

She reached over to pat her sister's hand. "Let's go see Ernie and get advice on what to do. I don't care about the TV and the other things they took, but I must get Joe's ring and Mother's necklace back. Maybe he has an idea on how. If not, we always have your plan of playing like Perry Mason or Jessica Fletcher."

They drove the rest of the way in silence. Betty quit crying. Clarence cleared the ever-present frog out of his throat. Leona found fault with everyone's driving. Didn't these people have jobs to go to or houses to stay in? Why were they all out on the roads getting in her way?

Around the next corner was the office of Ernie Lanyard, an old and trusted friend and lawyer who attended to her and Joe's affairs for years. He'd know what she needed to do next. When she parked in front of the building, everything looked the same, but Ernie's sign out front was gone. What was going on?

She helped the others out of the minivan, and they went inside Ernie's office. Paula, the woman who had been with Ernie for many years, wasn't sitting behind the receptionist desk. In her place was an older teenager wearing a blouse that was too low in the front and a skirt that was too high all the way round. She stared at them like her mind was on vacation.

"Where's Paula?" Leona asked. "Did she finally retire?"

"Who?" The girl fanned her store-bought eyelashes as she looked at them.

"Paula Burnoff. You know, Ernie's secretary."

"Well, I don't know anything about a Paula, but Mr. Lanyard isn't here anymore. He sold his business to my boss, Tristan Wilcox. Would you like to see him?"

"What do you mean Ernie's not here?" Leona hoped to spark some sign of brain activity in the young girl's face. "Ernie's been here for over 30 years. How could he up and leave without saying anything to anyone?"

The young lady shrugged, making her long earrings sway a little. "Mr. Lanyard's been gone for several months." She glanced around nervously before staring at Leona. "Um—when he found out he had cancer and didn't have much time left, he moved to be near his daughter in Cleveland. He sold his office and his practice to Tristan—er, Mr. Wilcox."

Leona crossed her arms. "But why didn't someone inform me of this? Ernie's been my lawyer for years. I should have been notified about his leaving."

"We've only been open a few days, and we haven't made it through all the files left behind. What did you say your name was?" She started digging through a pile of file folders on her desk.

"Walker. Leona Walker."

The young thing sat back in her chair. "That explains it. We're only up to the letter L in the files. I think W comes after that."

Leona gritted her teeth for a second as she tried to restrain her tongue. "As a former teacher, I can assure you W does indeed come after L." She turned to look at her companions. "Did you know anything about this?" Both shook their heads, so she turned back to the young lady. "What happened to Paula, Ernie's secretary?"

The young lady shrugged and avoided eye contact. "She retired, I guess. All I know is that I have the job now. Is there something you want?"

Leona turned again to look at Clarence and Betty with a roll of her eyes. "Oh, my word. Now what do I do?"

"Don't give up so easily. Talk to this Tristan person." Betty smiled at the young woman. "He's a lawyer too. Right, miss?"

"Oh yes, I've seen his diploma. He's a lawyer all right."

Leona smiled at the young thing. "Then I'd like to see him, if you please."

"He's not in right now—"

A man's voice sounded behind them. "Hello!" A young man walked in and closed the door behind him. Dressed in a cheap suit with his tie folded and hanging out of his jacket pocket, he extended his hand. "I didn't know anyone but Amber was here. Are you clients of Mr. Lanyard? I'm Tristan Wilcox. I'm taking over his practice." He shook hands with all three of them when they told him their names. "Why don't you come into my office and let's talk. Amber, can you get some bottled water for these folks?" He opened his office door and motioned for them to come in.

Leona didn't immediately move. She didn't want this kid. She wanted Ernie. The experience difference between the two must be light years. What did this kid know? He was probably fresh out of law school, and she needed someone who knew what he was doing. She fought the urge to turn and leave.

Tristan motioned again for them to come. Betty nudged Leona from behind. Leona let out a soft sigh and went inside the office. It looked the same as when Ernie was there, with a large, carved wooden desk and an oversized chair behind it. A matching wooden

39

table stood in front of a wall covered in reference books on wooden bookshelves. The tan carpet, to Leona's surprise, seemed threadbare. When Ernie was handling Joe's matters after his death, she'd thought Ernie kept a nice office. She must have been too preoccupied or bereaved to notice how old everything seemed.

Tristan got a chair from the table and placed it beside the two chairs in front of the desk before taking his seat. He folded his hands together. "I've only been here a couple of weeks and haven't had time to review all the files. I'm working hard to get up to speed on everything. Were you clients of Mr. Lanyard? Was there an issue he was working on for you?"

"Ernie was an old friend of my husband's," Leona began. "I need advice in a matter and thought he might help me. I hear he's not here anymore."

Tristan squirmed in his chair. "He left town suddenly and well, here I am." He held his hands wide with a big grin on his face.

Betty shook her head. "The young lady told us he had cancer and didn't have long to live." She found a tissue in her purse and wiped her eyes.

Tristan's hand covered the lower part of his face. "Yes. Well, that's the story..." His voice trailed off.

"Why didn't Nancy let us know about Ernie?" Betty twisted the tissue in her hand. "Poor Nancy. What will she do without Ernie?" She uncrumpled the tissue and blew her nose.

"Trust me, she'll do fine." Tristan leaned forward, his chair creaking with his movement, and whispered. "Were you really good friends?"

Leona lifted her eyebrows in surprise. "We grew up together. We're all hometown folks. Why do you ask?"

Tristan chuckled again and whispered, "He doesn't really have cancer. He ran off to Mexico with his secretary. His wife moved to Cleveland to be near their daughter." He sat back and crossed his arms.

The trio sat in their chairs without saying anything. Leona couldn't believe the last words uttered.

Clarence leaned forward and spoke the question rolling through Leona's mind. "Ernie ran off with Paula?" He started laughing, hard, like a man envious of another man's victory. "That Ernie! Who knew he had a thing for Paula? They'd been working together almost as long as he'd been married." He went into another spate of laughing.

Leona slapped her hand on the desk which made Clarence stop his outburst for a moment. "Clarence Brown, you're laughing about a man who deserted his wife and is living in sin. That's not funny! It's shameful!"

Clarence choked down his amusement and agreed with her.

Betty jumped in. "So, Nancy's all right? She's with her daughter? That's a relief. She would have a tough time facing anyone around here after what Ernie did."

Tristan, still smiling, glanced at Clarence. "Mr. Lanyard left her the title to this building and the divorce papers. Must have done it right before they left. He took their savings and left her the house and law office. She, in turn, sold the practice to me. For a decent price, I might add. She still owns the building and charges me rent. I was happy to walk into an established practice. Other than getting acquainted with clients, I hope things will stay just the way they were when Ernie was here."

Clarence cleared his throat. "If you want some advice from me, you might look for better clerical help. She might be good-looking, but she's not the sharpest pencil in the drawer."

Tristan laughed. "She's my cousin who wanted to earn a little money before going to beauty school. Since I needed someone to help me answer phones and man the office, I hired her. I'll advertise for a real law clerk when I can afford one. Now, what can I do for you?"

Leona moved to the front of her chair. "I'm the one with the problem. My house was robbed and ransacked, and I don't think the police are doing all they can to find my things. I wanted to know if you could make them search harder."

Tristan frowned while he mulled it over. "What do the police tell you they are doing?"

"Investigating." Leona felt antsy and started to rise but decided to stay sitting. "That's it. They're not rousting criminals or talking to their informants or..."

"How do you know they're not?"

"They haven't found my things yet."

"Crime investigations take time." Tristan leaned forward in his chair. "How long has it been since the robbery?"

Betty blurted out, "Three days."

Tristan's mouth fell open. "Three days? That's not much time. If they don't have any suspects, they will look at all aspects of the crime. Sometimes they solve it sooner, but I think tracking down burglars can take longer than three days."

"There's no time to lose. I need them to find the hoodlums now! This 'we're investigating' is not a satisfactory answer for me."

Clarence spoke up. "The detective called it an active investigation."

Tristan nodded as if he understood. "That's good. It means they're doing all they can to solve it." He looked at Leona. "Is there something in particular you want them to find?"

"The thieves have my husband's wedding band, and the detective told me that they sell gold jewelry to people who melt jewelry down. My Joe's gold wedding band. I want it back. Now." Leona felt like she was going to cry. "And my mother's ruby necklace. I want that back too."

The door opened, and the young receptionist walked in with four bottles of water. She put them on the desk and left. Tristan stood up and twisted the caps to open them and handed the bottles to his clients.

"The police are doing their jobs. You may think they're taking their time, but they're likely following their procedures for any burglary. The only thing you can do is wait and hope they find the criminals. The necklace and the ring, they're small items, easy to hide and hard to find." He pressed his lips together. "I'm sorry to say it, but I don't think they'll ever find them. You may need to accept that they're gone. You were insured, weren't you?"

His words cut right through her heart. "Insurance won't replace my Joe's ring." Leona rubbed her aching temples and heaved a heavy sigh. "So, there's nothing you can do to hurry it along?"

"Not really. I advise you to be patient. You could call them every few days and ask if there's been any progress. That might push them a little harder. Otherwise, you need to stay out of their way. Did you call your insurance agent?"

Leona sighed again. The lump in her throat was throbbing as much as her head was. "Yes, they are helping me with the cleanup and repairs. Yesterday I watched them carry the broken remains of my china cabinet out the door and put it into a dumpster." She paused to push the rising lump back down. "But I can't put a dollar value on things that are sentimental."

Tristan opened a drawer in his big wooden desk and pulled out a purse packet of tissues. He tossed them toward her side of the desk. His face reddened as he made several awkward moves to pick them up and set them down more gently. "I'm very sorry for your loss. You're right. Some things can never be replaced. I don't know what else to tell you other than say your prayers a miracle will happen."

It wasn't the answer Leona wanted to hear, but she realized the futility of pressing the issue. Ernie would have likely given the same advice. She thanked the kid and stood to go. "Send me a bill for your time. You should find me in your files when you get to the Ws."

"No charge," Tristan escorted them to the door. "I didn't do anything for you. Besides, it's nice to meet some of my clients." He leaned forward. "I feel I should make this clear. I specialize in corporate law, not criminal law. I can help you with insurance, real estate, or business issues, but I'm not sure I can be of much help regarding the felonious issues of this case."

Leona pursed her lips. "Maybe you should do some research about it. In a small town like this, we need a jack-of-all-trades lawyer." She helped Clarence get to his feet. "Thanks for your time." Tristan shook hands as they went out.

Back in the minivan, Betty buckled her seatbelt. "He's a nice young man. I think he'll be a great lawyer."

"You would," Leona turned into the street toward home. "I have to admit, he's nice looking, but I'm not sure how much he can do. Let's talk about that plan of yours, Betty."

CHAPTER 5

When they pulled into the driveway, Leona was surprised to see the coffee group waiting on them. Irene was on the porch swing with Carly, seemingly deep in conversation. Their husbands conversed under the boxelder tree in the front yard. Nick looked bored as George talked on his cell phone. He waved to them as they drove up the driveway.

Leona parked beside the large dumpster sitting behind Joe's Eldorado. The day before, the three-man crew made good progress in the clean-up, but it had been heart wrenching for Leona to listen to the clanging, crashing, and banging noises as they threw her belongings and shattered mementos into the dumpster.

Irene came down the ramp as Leona turned off the minivan. "We should have called earlier, but we assumed you'd be here cleaning up. We came to help you." She went to the other side of the minivan to help with Clarence's walker.

Betty's cane beat a quick tempo on the concrete. "We were checking on the police to make sure they are working hard to find our things."

"And are they?" Irene asked as Carly walked up.

47

"It's under investigation." Clarence wheeled his loud walker toward the ramp.

"Active investigation," Betty added as Nick and George joined them.

Carly wore a white blouse under a loose vest that hung over her leggings. Leona felt the side of her nose start to crinkle. For someone who prided herself on being an interior decorator, her ability to pick an outfit to clean in was either atrocious or very intentional. Her manicured nails had probably never seen anything stronger than hand soap, and Leona doubted today would be any different.

"Nick can oil that squeak for you, Clarence." Carly gave him a wink as he walked by her.

"What squeak?" Without a pause, Clarence marched up the ramp.

"I don't hear anything either." Nick ignored his wife's stern look and followed Clarence.

Carly cheeks reddened under her makeup. She opened her mouth to say something, but on this rare occasion, decided against it.

Betty shoved a large box into Carly's hands and told her to bring it. She gave Betty a glare of fire before following everyone else to the porch. Betty returned to the van and got Prissy out of her cat carrier before leading her on her leash up the ramp.

Leona hurried up the ramp to unlock the new front door's deadbolt. With the door opened wide, she walked onto the subflooring of the living room. The holes in the wall were patched, and a fresh coat of paint made it seem nothing had happened. In the kitchen, the dishes, pots, pans, utensils, silverware, Tupperware, and other non-destructible items sat on the countertops waiting to be sanitized. "The house is a mess." Leona pushed the silverware aside so Carly could put the box down.

Irene bounced on her toes. "That's why we're here. Let's get this party on the road!"

Carly's smoothed her white blouse. "Nick said we might help you repaint the walls, but I see that's already been done. And we don't lay carpet so we can't help with that. There isn't anything for us to do."

The smug look on Carly's face nipped at Leona's sassiness. "The insurance company paid for a crew to repaint the damaged walls but—"

"Good! You won't need us then. Come on, Nick."

"—but there's still a lot of cleaning left to do. I'd appreciate your help with that."

Carly licked her lips and looked down at her manicured nails. "Well, I..." She tugged on the bottom of her vest.

"We need all the help we can get." Betty let Prissy go, and the cat made a beeline for her person's bedroom. "The faster we get it done, the faster things will be back to normal. But first, let's test our new coffee pot. We got it just this morning. I found a few cookie tins in the garage freezer where the hoodlums didn't look. I'm happy for that."

"Is that where you keep your cold hard cash?" Nick snickered after he uttered the words. The ladies faked laughs at the less-than-clever pun, and the men groaned.

Leona moved kitchenware around so they could plug in the coffeemaker. "George Junior told us we should get new carpet later this week."

Carly crossed her arms and tilted her head. "That's wonderful. Plus, you'll have new furniture and all new things. I wish our house had been robbed!" Her wide sparkling eyes looked all around the room.

The group fell silent. Nick shook his head.

Irene came to the rescue by changing the subject. "Did you get a list for the insurance company?" After Leona nodded, she added, "That must have been hard."

Grateful her friend had the good sense to move the attention from Carly, Leona pushed it farther away. "Yes, we spent all day yesterday going through things. The crew threw out the broken stuff plus the stuff I'll never use again, like our clothes, towels, toiletries, and such. The thought of filthy hooligans having their hands on our personal stuff—well, I could never wear it again so out it went."

Irene nodded. "I would feel the same way. But your kitchen items, you're okay with keeping them?"

"Bleach water and soap kills all the germs and what that doesn't get, heat will finish off when I cook. We ran a couple loads in the dishwasher yesterday." She waved her hand around the kitchen.

"It might be time to clean out the extra stuff and donate it somewhere."

"Coffee's ready!" Betty filled white foam cups with dark liquid, and Irene handed them out. "Grab some cookies, and let's go sit on the front porch out of the paint fumes."

"I'd go a thousand miles to get some of your delicious cookies, Betty." Clarence squeaked his way along. With a soft cry of triumph, he picked up two and placed them on the seat of his walker.

Leona was about to leave when she saw Carly peeking in her cupboards. She took a step toward Carly as she inspected another cabinet. A good slap on the hand might get the message across to stop snooping, but instead, she opened her mouth to tell her.

Betty came up behind Leona. "I'll make another pot of coffee, Leona. That might help us all be more respectful and less rude, don't you think?"

The words stopped Leona in her tracks and Carly from opening another door. "Yes, that's a good idea." Leona sent Carly, who had her hand on another cabinet handle, one of the looks she used to give her children when they misbehaved in public.

Carly's eyebrows rose. She brushed past Leona, got a coffee cup and cookie, and left the two sisters.

"Be nice," Betty whispered loudly to Leona.

"I'm trying."

On the porch, Carly sat in Leona's wicker chair. "Your old furniture was—well, old." Before Nick could take a breath, she went on. "I don't mean that in a bad way, but you really should

51

replace furniture every ten years, otherwise it's worn and full of dust mites." She took a bite of cookie. "Now you have the chance to get some nice furnishings. If you'd like, I can go with when you pick it out. I know the latest styles in décor and could make your house much nicer than it was before."

If Leona bit her tongue any harder, she might have bit it in two. Suppressing her emotions to maintain civility in the group was about to give way to a maelstrom of angry responses that she'd probably regret tomorrow. Or the next day for sure.

An uncomfortable silence filled the air until Betty offered her opinion. "I've always liked the homey feel to Leona's house. Our problem now is making sure we decontaminate everything. We picked up buckets and bleach at the store this morning, but we left them in the back of the minivan. Irene, can you help me get those?"

Nick put down his coffee cup. "Carly and I will get them. Come on, Carly."

"I'm eating, Nick, dear." The last word came out like Prissy's hiss.

The cat at Betty's feet even lifted her head to look at Carly.

Nick stood and walked toward Carly. "You can finish after we get the cleaning supplies."

Carly pushed her sleeves up on her arms and furrowed her brow. Nick took her arm and pulled her out of the chair and down the ramp out of sight of the others.

The group who remained on the porch stared at each other. One of them let out a giggle and the others joined in, muffling their laughter as best as they could.

Irene rubbed her forehead. "Carly never learned the art of graciousness."

Betty tilted her head and got a faraway look in her eyes. "I wonder if they have classes for that?"

All humor had left Leona. "She'd probably flunk out."

"As our mother told us..." Betty gave a narrow-eyed glare to Leona, "...if you can't say anything nice about someone, don't say anything. Maybe Carly's mom never told her social manners." Her eyes widened. "Shhh, here they come."

Betty went in the house and brought out the coffee pot and started refilling cups. The rest started small conversations amongst themselves and raved about the treats, acting like they hadn't noticed anything out of the ordinary.

Carly and Nick walked up with the cleaning supplies. Carly's face was flushed, her lips pressed together as if holding in something ready to burst out. Nick maintained his cool in the wake of the hostility floating off his wife. They went straight into the house without speaking.

The uncomfortable situation made Leona's skin crawl. Irene remarked how delicious the cookies were and asked what carpet colors Leona was considering for the living room.

Nick and Carly rejoined the others and took their seats. Betty warmed their coffee and offered them more cookies. Whatever Nick told her had its desired effect. Carly's lips didn't part, not even to eat the rest of her cookie. An air of unease settled under the porch around the friends who usually got along so well.

Betty bent down and picked Prissy up to hold her close. "Anyone want to pet my cat?"

Leona turned up her nose. "You know I don't. That cat hates me."

"Prissy doesn't hate anybody. She just likes to play favorites." Betty stroked the yellow fur.

The rest declined the offer as well. As an uneasy peace settled in, Leona and Irene went into the kitchen, followed by the others. Nick put the buckets in the sink and filled them with hot bleach water. Carly opened a new package of sponges and put them in the water.

"Who's up for cleaning?" Leona wrung out the sponges and offered them to any volunteer.

Carly spoke up first. "Nick and I have to go. Sorry to bug out on the work, but I have an appointment that I can't miss. Come on, Nick." She turned on her heel and left.

Nick's face reddened. The muscles in his jaw worked as hard as his hands as he wrung out the other sponges. "She didn't tell me about any appointment, but I guess we must go. Should I come back later to help, Leona?"

Her heart went out to the poor man. He'd likely get back whatever he'd given earlier once their SUV doors were closed. "Can Carly leave you here and go to her appointment alone? I can take you home."

His jaw muscles quit working, and he froze for a second before his shoulders sagged. "She'll insist I go with her." He heaved a sigh and dried his hands off.

George patted his back. "Don't worry about it. The five of us can handle the cleaning. You have your hands full."

Nick gave a crooked grin and nodded before leaving. "See you at the coffee shop tomorrow."

The group watched until the SUV pulled away from the curb. "I'll start in the bathroom." Irene picked up a bucket of bleach water. She whistled a lively tune as she went down the hallway.

George filled the sink with more water and bleach and started wiping the kitchen cabinets out. Leaving Clarence and Betty to do what they wanted, Leona took a bucket and went to her own bathroom.

Carly's words kept ringing through her head. They'd stung more than she'd let anyone know. Her decorating style had always been for comfort, not style. Her faded and worn sofa had withstood the family's popcorn fights, messy pizza parties, being used as a sickbed, and long movie nights. The memories woven into its fabric had been too strong to replace it. How would it feel seeing something new and different in its place?

Her attention went back to cleaning the master bath. With each swipe of the sponge, she washed away the germs and bad feelings, bugs, microbes, and cooties. She reclaimed her space and put things right. By the time she finished, she felt cleansed and lighter.

She looked in on Betty who was finished cleaning her bathroom. In the kitchen, George and Irene washed the last of the pots, pans, and utensils. Clarence sat on one of their bar stools, drying what was washed. The dishwasher was running, filled with plates, bowls, and silverware Clarence was happy not to have to dry.

Leona gathered the buckets and sponges and took them to the garage. The outside air was so fresh she took several deep breaths. Time to get her friends out in it. She went back into the house and the faint fumes and announced, "Finish what you're doing, and I'll take you out for supper."

Irene stepped back from the sink. "Good timing. I just washed the last spatula."

Still in their work clothes, Leona, Betty, George, Irene, and Clarence chose to eat at Prairie Air Diner where the burgers were good and the ambiance country. The group knew everyone dining there, and greetings were called out around the room. A waitress who had been in Leona's fourth grade class showed them to a table near the windows.

After they ordered, George said, "You'll be back in your house soon, Leona. How will it feel getting back to normal?"

Leona wished the question would die a slow death so she wouldn't have to answer it. Normal? Nothing about her house was normal and never would be again. Normal left her house when Joe died. The new normal people told her would come after his death perished at the hands of invaders. The new things were fine, but the history and memories her old possessions held would soon be interred at the dump. There was no such thing as normal anymore.

Betty kicked Leona under the table, drawing her out of her miseries. "Yes, it will be nice to be back home."

"But nothing for her will be normal until she gets Joe's ring back," Betty tilted her head and smirked. "She won't sleep until then. You know why?"

The waitress brought their orders and asked if they needed anything else. When told all was well, she hurried away to another table.

"Are you going to tell us?" Irene ate one of her fries.

"At night," Betty started, waving her own fry around to make her point, "she puts Joe's ring on the pillow next to her. Says it makes her feel like he's still there and she sleeps better. Isn't that the sweetest thing you ever heard?" Her eyes filled with tears as the fry went into her mouth.

Leona's face grew hotter than the sizzling meat in front of her. Her reason for wanting the ring so badly was no one's business but hers. She gave her sister a glare, but Betty's eyes were on her food.

With a quick motion, Irene covered Leona's hand with her own. Her eyes glimmered with tears. "That's so sweet. No wonder you're feeling so bad. I don't blame you."

"I'll find it yet."

Clarence cleared his throat. "At the same time, the police know what they're doing. You don't. Let them do their jobs." He stabbed the air with his own fry.

This using fries as point makers was making Leona's blood boil, then hearing Clarence defend the lack of action on Smythe's part almost pushed her over the edge. She took a drink of her iced tea hoping it would cool her insides. "But they'll ruin the ring if we don't find it soon. You heard Smythe say it. They melt down things like that into a blob so they can make other things. The sooner the police find the ring, the less likely they'll have destroyed it."

Beside her, Irene gasped. "Melt it? George, isn't there something you can do? You have connections at the police station. Get them to find Joe's ring."

"Dear, it's not that easy. I'm sure if they knew where it was, they'd bring it back to her. I'm afraid Smythe is right. The ring is probably gone for good."

A shuffle under the table preceded a cry of pain from George and a stern look from Irene. It made Leona want to melt into her seat.

Betty's mouth was full of food but that didn't keep her from expressing her opinion. "You should have given it to Brett after Joe died, just like I told you to. If you had, the ring would be safe and sound with him."

Feeling like she was about to erupt, Leona took another drink of iced tea. "Maybe I should have, but I wasn't ready to pass it along yet. That ring is MINE, and I want it back!"

The restaurant suddenly became quiet, and Leona realized she had used her angry teacher's voice. Her food became unappealing, and she pushed her plate toward the middle of the table.

Betty clapped her hands. "Prissy loves it when I bring food home for her. She will love that twelve-dollar hamburger. Silly cat, loves all the trimmings too." She giggled as she pulled the plate toward her.

No way! Leona yanked her plate back in front of her and took a big bite of the hamburger. That silly cat was not getting her expensive meal. The table of friends snickered as they ate heartily. It helped Leona's heart to relax a little. She would keep searching for Joe's ring, but if she failed, she had a good support system to catch her.

CHAPTER 6

"It will be nice to sleep in our own beds tonight." Betty packed the last of their things in the hotel room two days later. She prowled around the room making sure they'd left nothing behind. "What are you doing?"

"I'm making a list of places to go shopping today. George called this morning. The insurance company has issued a check for the replacement of our broken dishes, TV, and other things that were taken. I'll call Jennifer later and ask her to order a new computer for us. She knows more about them than I do."

"Let's get a really big TV so we can read the captions better." Betty zipped her bag shut. "And the furniture store. We need chairs to watch TV."

"It's at the top of my list. But first, I thought we could start checking out a few pawnshops for Mother's necklace. I made a list of them to visit."

Betty wrinkled her nose. "Pawnshops? Aren't they kind of seedy places to go?"

"I don't know. I've never been to one, but I'm not going to sit here and do nothing while the police increase patrols and keep their eyes open. I'm going hunting for my ring and necklace."

Leona closed the window on her phone and looked at her list. "My goodness, who knew we had so many pawnshops spread across town."

A light knock at the door told them the cleaning woman had arrived. As Leona finished the last of her coffee, Betty went to the door and opened it. It wasn't the cleaning lady standing there, but Smythe, decked out in a business suit.

"Oh! It's you!" Betty stepped aside so Leona could see.

Smythe took a step inside the doorway. "I'm sorry to barge in on you like this. Mr. Brown told me you were here."

Leona covered her heart with her hand. "We thought you were someone else. We're checking out and moving back home today. Please come in." Waving an invitation to him, she pointed to the small sofa in the corner. Betty placed a cup with the last of their coffee in front of him before sitting in the other chair. Leona sat on the edge of the bed, feeling as tense as Prissy seemed in her cage.

Leona stared at Smythe as he looked around the room. He was a handsome young man. Well dressed, he was neatly groomed and clean-shaven, and seemingly well mannered. On the outside, he looked like someone she might consider introducing to her oldest granddaughter if they were closer in age. But why were his hands trembling? Was something bothering him, or did he have too much coffee this morning? She wanted to ask but pushed the feeling away. He was in charge of the investigation. Torquing him off would slow what little progress he was making on her case.

"What brings you here today?"

He made a sound of approval after he tasted Betty's coffee. Undoing his jacket button, he turned to Leona. "I was gruff with you the other day, and I wanted to apologize. I had a difficult day, but that's no excuse for how I acted. I stopped by to see if you had any other questions I could answer."

Leona lightly tapped her pen on her thigh. "Have you found anything yet?"

"This coffee is a lot better than the stuff at the office." He took another sip. "No, we haven't found anything yet, but we're hopeful. I know you are particularly interested in finding a ruby necklace and a gold wedding band, right?"

Betty jumped in. "Poor Leona has been despondent over the loss of those items. Do you know what she does with that ring? It will break your heart!"

"Betty!" Leona's teacher voice filled the room. "The detective isn't interested in those trivial stories. He's a busy man. Aren't you."

He nodded as he sipped more coffee. "This is mighty fine coffee." He surveyed the cup as he held it up. "You even have the same china pattern we have at the office." He chuckled at his own attempt at humor.

Leona was not amused but forced a faked smile on her face. "Betty has a knack for making good coffee. And good cookies. Once we get settled, she can start baking again and restock her supplies." She eyed him to see if he would react. He didn't. "You said you were hopeful. Does that mean you are hot on the trail of the culprits?"

He clinched his fist slightly and worked a muscle in his jaw. "We're doing the best we can. As I told you, there's been a rash of burglaries around town in the past year. We think there's a well-organized burglary ring in town, but we haven't nailed down who the leader is yet. He's the one we want, so we have to be careful not to scare him off. If he runs like a rabbit, we'll never be able to close the cases."

Leona watched his fists get tighter and the jaw muscle was working harder. He seemed more intent on the coffee than most people would have been. She watched him swallow hard. Gradually, his features softened and appeared under control.

"And what about my ruby necklace and gold band?"

"As I told you before, they're small and can be easily hidden until they're melted down for their precious metals content."

Leona's brain froze on hearing the dreaded words again. Melted down! The ring would be gone forever. Just like Joe. She would have to face his loss every night, alone in that empty bed. With the unused pillow beside her. She couldn't bear to think of it. Her heart felt heavy which made it hard for her to breathe.

He continued. "Odds are we'll never find them. I hope our finding the theft ring will make up a little for your loss. Catching them means no one else will lose their assets." He tipped his head back, then put down an empty cup. "I mainly stopped by to see if you had serial numbers we could track. On your TV and computer."

Leona blinked away the moisture gathered in her eyes. "Serial numbers?" Leona pushed her worries from her mind. "I've been so concerned with the cleanup I hadn't thought of them. I think we wrote serial numbers on the operation manuals. They didn't take anything from my desk drawers. I'll look for those when we get home and bring them to you by tomorrow at the latest."

"That would be an immense help to us. If they show up in a pawnshop or the newspaper, we'll know who took them in."

"So you're looking in pawnshops?"

His hand movements became slower and more deliberate. "Rarely do they show up there because pawnshop owners require proof of ownership from the person bringing the item in. They take photos and submit information to us to compare against the stolen goods list. Even then, not a lot of stolen merchandise goes through the pawnshops. Most is sold through the black market."

Betty piped up. "Black market? Here? I thought they only had those in third world countries." She leaned toward Smythe. "I've always wondered, are there other colors of markets?"

The sound of a vacuum cleaner running down the hall provided background for the seconds of silence. Leona stared at Betty, wondering what prompted such a silly question.

Smythe sat still, open-mouthed. He folded his hands together. "As far as I know, there're no other colors of illegal markets. The black market can be anywhere. All it takes is a man on the street opening his coat and asking if you want to buy one of the watches hanging in it."

"I thought those people were called flashers?"

Leona clapped her hands together to stop Betty's inane inquiries. "Never mind! Let's not go there. Do you need anything else, Smythe?"

Smythe fought to hide a grin. "No, the serial numbers will aid our search. I'll be in touch. Ladies, thanks for the coffee. It was delicious." Leona held the door for him as he left.

She leaned against the closed door and looked at Betty. "I wonder what his real reason was for coming?"

"Why are we driving here?" Clarence asked in the whiny high-pitched voice of a child wanting to go out to play. "Smythe said they're checking the pawnshops."

"I'm helping out the police." Leona's hands firmly gripped the wheel. Smythe's visit that morning had spurred her to action. She was convinced his mention of wanting to find the head of the burglary ring meant little time was being spent on her individual case.

She pulled into the parking lot of a dingy pawnshop and parked alongside several other cars. The bars over the windows and fading paint didn't give a come-on-in look to the place. Litter of all sorts lay along the foundation of the building and against the fence in the back. The grungy look of the lone person smoking beside an Employees-Only side door put her off, but nothing would keep her from her mission. Finding a parking spot near the front door, she stopped and told Betty and Clarence, "Stay here to make sure nothing else gets stolen. I'll be right back."

"Do hurry!" Betty cried out just before the door slammed.

Leona smoothed her new polyester slacks and blouse and felt her hair to make sure it was in place. Her heart was beating fast as she opened the door and stepped inside. To her surprise, the interior was clean and neat. A multitude of musical instruments lined one wall, with electronic equipment displayed inside the glass case in front of them. In the middle of the room, diamond jewelry sparkled under the fluorescent lights in another glass case. On the other end of the store, guns of all makes and calibers lined the wall and display case. Bicycles, power tools, and a myriad of items were lined up along the big windows at the front of the store and along the aisles toward the back.

A lady behind the jewelry counter called out, "May I help you, ma'am?" She gave Leona a good customer-service smile.

Walking to the display case, Leona's eyes were drawn to the sparkling diamonds of the many wedding ring sets in the case. On the other end of the case, a young couple were bent over the selection, pointing and whispering. Scanning for anything familiar, she replied, "I'm looking for a necklace of mine that was stolen from my house several days ago."

Silence filled the store as everyone turned to look at her. A frown replaced the smile on the clerk's face. She replied loudly enough for the other customers to hear, "We don't accept stolen items in this store. We work closely with the police department to make sure none of our merchandise is hot."

The man behind the gun counter came up beside the clerk with narrowed eyes that left no doubt that he wouldn't allow such rumors to spread. "Who told you we sell stolen goods?"

Leona felt her face redden, and her racing heart urged her to turn and run. She looked down at her shuffling feet, then looked the man. "No one! I didn't mean to imply that you did. I'm acting out of desperation to find something precious to me, and I didn't know where else to look. The police indicated they are checking pawnshops, and I thought I'd help them out."

The man's eyes relaxed a little. "We work with our highly effective police department, not private citizens. I suggest you go home so you don't bother our customers."

Leona took a step back. "I'm sorry, I didn't mean to imply anything untoward about your business. I apologize if I did." She expressed her regret in a loud voice so the other customers would hear her apology. Leona studied the man's face. Less hostility seemed to be there. Maybe he wouldn't kick her out for good if she asked one more question. She leaned in closer to him and spoke softly. "Maybe you can still help me. Can you tell me where I might find stolen items? Is there a black marketplace that I might visit?"

Titters around the store told Leona she'd asked a silly question in too loud of a whisper. She apologized loudly again. "Look, the thieves took my mother's necklace and my late husband's wedding band. I must get them back, and I don't know where else to look."

The man's narrowed eyes returned. She'd done enough damage. It was time for her to flee. "I—I should have never come here." She turned to go with what little dignity she had left.

"Wait!" the man called after her.

Leona stopped. She closed her eyes as she tried to decide whether to stay or keep going. Betty and Clarence were probably counting the minutes in the minivan, wondering when she would return. But what other chance might she have to get information? She opened her eyes and turned around.

The man drummed his fingers on the glass counter. "We can go talk in my office. Darcie, you and Jason take over for a few minutes." He held his arm out to direct her way.

Whispering and soft giggling followed Leona to the office door. She entered a small but neat office in the back of the shop. Papers with lists, sticky notes, and posters of guns wallpapered the office. Two filing cabinets filled an already small space behind the desk. She took a seat in the folding chair in the corner. Her knees brushed against the front of the desk as she sat there.

The man sat behind the desk and looked at her. "Ever been in a pawnshop before?"

Leona shook her head.

"I didn't think so. Listen, Mrs.—"

"Walker. Leona Walker."

"Mrs. Walker. You seem confused so I'll be straight with you. We pawnshop dealers work hard to stay within the law. We're not criminals. We're businessmen trying to run our legal businesses so we can support our families and help other people out of tight spots. Like I told you, we work closely with cops when they're looking for stolen goods. Here, I'll show you." He pulled a desk drawer open and pulled out a pile of papers. "Here's a list of what they're looking for." He flipped through the stack, then handed a few to her to examine. She quickly scanned the photos and descriptions given. She handed them back.

He continued as he straightened them and put them back in the drawer. "We take photos of things people bring in and compare them to this list. Or we send the photos of the larger merchandise and information to the police department. Sometimes, law enforcement will stop in to look around and talk. We work hand-in-hand with them in trying to find stolen merchandise. Not much shows up here because crooks know what we do and know we'll report them if something turns up."

Leona looked at the purse in her lap. "I didn't realize."

"And as far as a black market goes, that's usually underground. You know what that means? It's not really a place as much as it's an activity that's hard to pin a location on. It's all very secret, in back alleys or dives. They're not places someone like you should go poking around, and certainly not the kind of people a lady should keep company with. Understand?"

Leona rubbed her furrowed brow, trying to soothe the tension out of it. "Of course. I'm not a total idiot but my desperation makes me look like one. I'm sorry to bother you."

The man sat back in his chair. "You seem like a nice lady." He cleared his throat. "Don't let your emotions get you into trouble. There's a lot of bad people out there, and I wouldn't want you to go someplace where you might get hurt. My advice is for you to go home and let the police handle it."

"There's no other advice you can give me on where to look?"

The man rolled a pencil on the desk, then rolled it back. He leaned forward across the desk. "Try the flea market on this side of Rapid City. They don't always check stuff there like we do. Maybe—and I ain't promising anything—maybe they might know something. But be careful! A lot of dubious characters work behind the scenes in those places. You could get into trouble real fast."

Leona perked up. "The flea market. The big one out on the highway? I've never been there, but it sounds like a place I could casually look around."

The man started to roll his eyes, but quickly rubbed them to hide it. "I don't recommend it. Take someone with you if you decide to go and watch your back. Don't announce why you're there or why you're looking. You mention stolen goods, and everyone will clam up." The man leaned back. "You carry a gun?"

Leona gasped. "No! Of course not."

A surprised look came across his face. "Listening to you talk—I mean, I assumed you being a southern lady meant you probably did. You might consider it. I have some nice ones for sale. There's lots of places to learn how to use one and take care of it."

Leona shook her head and stood to go. "I'm not a southern lady—I mean I'm a lady, and I've lived in Red Creek for over fifty years, but my Texas heritage has never been completely uprooted. Oh, never mind that. I've never carried a gun in my life and have no intention of starting now. Those things scare me." She stood to go. "Thanks anyway. I'll take friends with me. No one would hurt a group, right?"

The man made a doubtful expression, shook his head but offered nothing more. Leona thanked him for his time and advice and left.

CHAPTER 7

The coffee group met at the Bluebird Coffee Shop the next morning. The shop's comfy sofas and chairs and the smell of coffee in the air provided the perfect climate in which to solve the world's and other people's problems.

Leona carried her coffee to where the rest of the group sat. Betty, Clarence, George, and Irene sat in their usual places on the chairs and sofa. Nick and Carly were still in line to order. Since they came in together and no scowls were present, the group assumed they remained married.

Irene held her bagel up close to her mouth. "You must be happy to be home again. Is everything in order? Have you picked out furniture?" She took a big bite.

Leona sipped her coffee before answering. "We got a check from the insurance, so we went shopping."

"And we restocked the kitchen with everything I need to make cookies," Betty bounced in her seat. "I'm so happy to be able to cook again. I can't do without my kitchen."

George put his coffee on the coffee table "Was the carpet put in?"

"Yes. We're shopping for living room furniture later today, but don't tell Carly. I hope we find something that will suit me, not her. We have lawn chairs set up until we get something more comfortable."

The group greeted Nick and Carly as they sat down, completing the circle. Carly's presence subdued the group somewhat, so they sat in silence for a moment.

George wiped his hands and mouth on a napkin to clean off the icing from his donut. He leaned back on the overstuffed leather couch and propped his large latte on his overstuffed belly. "Have the police found the thieves yet?"

Leona shook her head and told them of her frustration at the police. She told them of her visit to the pawnshop and the suggestion of the owner to get a gun. The group voiced its appall and reminded her that having a gun and Betty in the same house might be trouble.

Betty heaved a big sigh as she rolled her eyes. "I know how to work a gun."

"That's what worries me, sister." Leona gritted her teeth. Her intent wasn't to hurt Betty, but she had no business being around a loaded weapon. "We've done fine all these years without one. No need to give thieves something dangerous to steal."

"So, what are you going to do?" Nick asked as he bit into his cinnamon roll.

"Go hunt for the thieves by myself." Leona sat back in her chair to watch the reaction to that statement.

"Oh, you can't do that." Carly fiddled with her beaded necklace. "You know nothing about chasing down criminals. You might get hurt! Why don't you offer a reward or something? That's an easier way to get your stuff back."

Betty nearly spilled her coffee in excitement as she waved her arm for attention. "We could offer my cookies as a reward. People have told me they'd do anything to have a few of my cookies. Thieves like cookies as much as regular people." She put the last piece of the store-bought cookie in her mouth, then brushed the crumbs from her lap.

The idea illuminated possibilities for Leona. Not the cookies, but cash. She scolded herself for not thinking of it before. By offering as much as a pawnshop or the black market and the guarantee that no questions would be asked, maybe the thieves would return the necklace and the ring.

A huge smile spread across Leona's face that brought everyone's eyes to her. "Carly, what a fabulous idea! I'll do it! How big of a reward do you think we should offer?"

Betty put down her coffee cup. "I think two dozen would be plenty—no! Spare no expense. Make it three dozen. Who could resist that?" Betty nodded her head.

Leona frowned at Betty. "I meant money. How much money should I put up for a reward?"

Betty's bottom lip came out. "You don't want my cookies?"

Leona patted her hand. "I'm not sure your reputation as the world's best cookie maker has reached the criminal sector yet. Let's use money."

Betty's lip still stuck out.

"We'll use your cookies to sweeten the pot and make our offer more irresistible. Together, they speak everyone's language."

Giggles were muffled by hands or bites into the donuts as Betty beamed.

Nick leaned forward to put his elbows on his knees. He spread his hands out. "How much are you willing to pay?"

Leona calculated in her head. She had a little in savings in the bank, but that was her emergency fund. Her investments and IRAs were reserved for supplementing her Social Security income and paying for her nursing home if needed. Taking care of Betty was more expensive than she'd thought it would be with hauling her all over town and endlessly buying groceries for her kitchen hobbies. She wasn't rich, only comfortable. "Maybe two hundred dollars. Do you think that's enough?"

"Are you kidding?" Carly smirked. "You have to give more than what the items are worth, otherwise the criminals have no incentive to return them. If they get more than two hundred dollars on the black market, they'll sell them there."

"What are they worth on the black market?"

Carly shrugged and went back to eating.

Everyone in the group nodded except for Irene. "Carly's right. For jewelry, I bet most rewards are more than that. George, we could pitch in a little, couldn't we?" George's eyes widened for a split second as a tinge of red spread across his face. He nodded reluctantly while staring at his coffee mug.

Leona noted the change in George. "I wouldn't hear of it. I don't want to owe anything to anyone. I think my best bet is to visit the flea market. That doesn't cost anything, and we can ask a few questions and see if we get anywhere. If something looks promising, I'll mention a reward."

Carly leaned forward. "I hear it's a creepy place. You might want to take some pepper spray with you. You could get attacked—"

"Where'd you hear that?" Nick brushed crumbs off his lap. "It's a marketplace where people are trying to make a living. What's so creepy about that?"

Carly crossed her arms and assumed her high-brow look. "I hear things. People who've been there told me. A lot of bad stuff goes on behind the tents and buildings. Drug addicts and cartels gather there."

Nick intertwined his fingers. "Not sure what kind of people you talk to, Carly, but I think that Leona should go and find out what she can. They have security officers around there. If it were unsafe, the police would have closed it down a long time ago."

Betty giggled. "She can be just like Jessica Fletcher from that TV show, *Murder She Wrote*. You know, doing her own investigations and asking the right questions. It was my idea to do that."

"To solving the mystery!" Irene raised her mug in salute.

Leona watched silently as the tittering, chuckling, and excited chatter passed around the group. While her mission may have seemed trivial to them, she was deadly serious about finding Joe's ring. Her mother's necklace, she could let go of without much more grieving, but she wouldn't let go of Joe's ring without a fight.

"Maybe you should have taken the pawn shop man up on his offer of a gun," Betty whispered to Leona as they walked down the aisles at the flea market a few hours later. "I didn't like the looks of that man selling the sweatshirts back there."

They walked close together ahead of Clarence who stopped to look at used books. Betty hooked her arm into Leona's as they strolled along the crowded marketplace. With so many people pushing to look at the vendors, it was hard to stay side by side.

"Don't be silly, Betty! We don't need a gun. Nick was right. These people have enterprises selling knickknacks, tee shirts, and vegetables. I don't see the criminal sort here. I think whoever Carly has been talking to is flat out wrong."

"I think it's creepy. And dirty." Betty brushed at dust gathering on her slacks. "My shoes will need a good cleaning when we get home."

"We'll look at all the booths, then go home. I'm beginning to think that man at the pawnshop sent us on a wild goose chase just to get me out of his office. I haven't seen anyone selling old jewelry." She stopped to pick up a ripe, plump tomato. "This looks delicious!"

"It might be injected with drugs," Betty whispered loudly.

The woman behind the table shot them a look that would burn leather. "What did you say?" she shouted above the din as she moved toward her booth's opening where she could confront the two wide-eyed women.

Leona pushed Betty behind her. "Um—she said this tomato must be envied by bugs." She held the tomato in front of her face and tried to focus on it. "Looks delicious!" She held it out to the woman with her best smile and picked up another tomato. "I'll take these two. They're full of wonderful nutrients. Yummy nutrients that are good for me." Her voice trailed off at the end.

The vendor gave a final, fiery glare, then took the tomatoes from Leona's hand. She stomped back into her booth and put them on a scale.

Leona prayed for patience and understanding as she paid, took the tomatoes, and thanked the frowning woman. She pulled Betty along with her. "I should have left you at home. That woman was ready to clobber both of us. Keep your comments to yourself."

"Carly said—"

"Carly doesn't have a clue what she's talking about. Just keep quiet." She looked behind them, standing on her tiptoes to peer through the growing crowd. "Where's Clarence? I thought he was right behind us."

Betty moved beside her to look around and past people. "I think he's stuck talking to that man about his books."

"There's no room in his house for more books, but I doubt that will stop him from buying more." Leona pulled her sister through the other market visitors. "He'll probably toss them on the pile of newspapers on the floor along with the other clutter." Leona shook her head. How he could live like that, she'd never understand. Since his wife died, the once-neat home had become a cluttered mess.

Leona made her way along the dusty rows of vendors, looking for anyone who might be selling jewelry. Trinkets of every kind, tee shirts with inappropriate messages, hats of every sort, food booths, farmers' produce, and antiques were everywhere. Most of the things, in her opinion, was just stuff. Nothing here would draw her back after they left, unless the tomatoes were as good as they looked.

One booth of antiques had a glass case and as Leona drew near, she could see jewelry inside. She shed Betty from off her arm before going into the booth. Opening her purse, she pulled out the old photo of her mother wearing the necklace and showed it to the meek, spectacled, short man. "I'm looking for a necklace just like this one. It's to be a gift to my niece for her wedding. Do you have anything like it?"

The man's gruff-looking wife snatched the photo from Leona's hand. "I'm in charge of the jewelry. Lemme look at it." She held the photo up close to her face, then shook her head. "No, we ain't got nothing like that. We got some other pretty ones though. Your niece might like them." She waved her hand toward the glass case.

"Um, no thanks. I want a necklace similar to this one for sentimental reasons." Leona got her photo back and quickly tucked it away in her purse. "Do you have any gold bands for men that you have recently purchased?"

The lady shook her head. "Not since last month." She pounded her large index finger on the glass case. "Look over what we got. There're some nice ones here."

Leona glanced over the selection. Most of them seemed rather new, not worn like Joe's ring. She mentioned this to the lady.

"Our customers want new-looking rings. The old ones, well, nobody wants 'em so we sell them to the gold people. I think they melt them so they can make new rings outta them."

Leona gasped and clutched at her heart. Her treasured connection to Joe may be in some golden blob in a back room somewhere. Desperation and heartache almost forced a cry of anguish out of her, but she swallowed it. She turned to go and nearly ran into Betty who was right behind her.

"Come with me." Betty went quickly, weaving in and out between people past a furniture vendor and another antique dealer. Betty kept tugging Leona until they reached a jewelry vendor at the end of an aisle. Betty excitedly pointed to several wood-and-glass display cases full of costume and gemstone jewelry. "Maybe it's here."

The sisters held on to each other as they walked along each glass case, carefully looking at the variety of gold wedding bands and necklaces, some of which looked old and worn, but none looked like Joe's band or her mother's necklace.

A man with a Dallas Cowboys tee shirt that barely covered his bulbous belly came up to the ladies. The tattoos on his arms ran all the way up his arms and into his sleeves. "Sumpin' you wanna see?" He cocked his hip and Leona wondered if just one leg could hold up all that weight.

"We're only looking for now." She stared at the tattoo on his neck, trying to figure out what it depicted. "If we find something that interests us, I'll let you know."

Tattoo Man walked back to his seat at the rear of his booth and kept a close eye on them.

The pair turned back to the case to look among the many necklaces inside. While Betty looked through the necklaces, Leona studied the several dozen men's wedding bands, hoping against hope she'd see Joe's ring. She looked at each one again in case she missed one. Disappointed again, she stepped back from the case. "At least there are gold bands around. I guess we keep looking." She turned to leave the booth.

Betty grabbed her sister's arm and pulled her back. "They have more. Look over here."

Tattoo Man eyed them as they walked past his display of colored glassware and delicate figurines. A cane-bottom chair and a marble top table sat beside a china cabinet that held mishmash of jewelry, thimbles, and small objects.

They pored over the assortment of items until Betty pointed to a blue bead necklace near the back. "Isn't that the necklace I gave you for Christmas one year? It had an odd clasp and see here? That one has the same kind. In fact, I think it's yours!"

Leona followed where she was pointing and gasped. If it wasn't hers, it was an exact replica. Her heart skipped a beat as she frantically searched through the other necklaces. Her mother's was nowhere to be seen. She waved at Tattoo Man who was feasting on what appeared to be a large mound of chili-covered French fries that had magically appeared from somewhere. He licked his fingers and wiped them dry on his shirt before he got up.

"Ya need something?" He let out a soft belch.

Leona tried hard not to wrinkle her nose or close her eyes in disgust. "Yes, please. That blue bead necklace in the back. Can I see that?"

Tattoo Man pulled a ring of keys from his pocket and fumbled through half of them before finding the one that would unlock the cabinet. With great ceremony, he pulled the necklace out and held it up between them. As it swung in his licked fingers, Leona and Betty leaned in for a closer view. Leona pushed the beads around with her fingernail.

"This looks just like a necklace I used to have." She looked up at Tattoo Man. "How much is it?" She looked at the tiny tag, then dug in her purse to start looking for her magnifying glass.

"Tag says it's $10. Nice piece of costume jewelry. It would look good on you."

Betty stood as tall as she could. "That's what I said when I bought it for her."

Tattoo Man frowned.

Leona punched her sister to hush. "Yes, I'll take it, but I'm curious. Do you know where it came from? Where you got it?"

"Not really. I think my uncle got it from an estate sale somewhere. Why?"

"No reason." She pulled the photo of her mother out of her purse. "Do you have a necklace that looks like this? I want one for my niece. As a wedding present."

The man looked at it for a long time. "I'm not sure. Seems familiar." He looked through the jewelry in the case for a few minutes. "Hang here while I check the back." He kept the blue necklace and locked the case before leaving.

"That's my blue necklace!" Leona told Betty when he was out of earshot. "I'm sure of it. Maybe he has Joe's ring and Mother's necklace in the back. If they're not, I'll ask him again where he got it. Maybe we'll get a new lead to follow." Her throat emitted a giddy cackle that startled her and made Betty take a step back. Was she losing control of her emotions?

"Are you really going to pay him to get your blue necklace back?"

"Yes. It's only ten dollars, and he won't know we're suspicious." Leona tapped out an impatient rhythm with her fingernails on the top of the glass case. "Oh Lord, please let my treasures be back there."

Betty uttered an "Amen."

After a few minutes, the man came back and announced he couldn't find it. "I guess I's wrong about it. We don't got one like that. Everything we got is in the cases. Wanna look at anything else?"

"If I knew where your uncle got this blue necklace, I could contact that person to see if he or she had more jewelry. Could you find out where he got this? It's exactly what I'm looking for."

Tattoo Man stepped back and frowned. "He may not remember. He buys stuff from all kinds of people. People're always looking to sell stuff. You gonna buy the blue one or not?"

"I'll buy it if you tell me who he bought it from. In fact, I'll pay you $20 for it, if you give me that information."

Shuffling his feet, Tattoo Man tilted his head and peered out the side of his narrowed eyes. "Why you gotta know that?"

"Because this is MY necklace that was stolen from me last week. And I want the thug who stole it from me!" Leona stopped, horrified at herself for using her bad-day teacher's voice. The floodgates of aggravation had opened and rushed out all at once before she could stop it. She slapped her hand over her mouth and sucked in a deep breath through her nose. "I'm sorry. I'm not blaming or accusing you or your uncle. My mother's necklace was in the same box as the blue necklace you have here. All I want is my mother's necklace and my husband's wedding ring." Leona felt herself shouting and tried to quiet her volume. The man was twice her size, but she wasn't backing down.

A crowd had gathered around the booth to watch. They murmured to each other, staring as Leona gripped the jewelry case. Was she going to tip it over? Would she break the glass? They were ready for her to give them a show.

Betty tugged at Leona's arm to pull her back a little. Seeing the surprise in the large man's eyes change into fire signaled she had pushed this beast as far as he was going to budge. Yanking her arm away from Betty, Leona regained her composure. She lowered her voice enough so only Tattoo Man could hear her. "I don't care about the other stuff the thieves took. I just want the two items back. Get them for me or tell me who you got the blue necklace from, so I can see if they have my ring and necklace. Please." She blinked, took a step back, and held out a $20 bill. "I promise not to talk to the police about where I found the bead necklace."

The side of Tattoo Man's nose crinkled as he met her stare and leaned in. Her own nose wanted to crinkle too as the smell of chili came on his breath. "I told you, lady. My uncle didn't say where he got it."

His inflection on the word "uncle" told her volumes. Leona stood as tall as she could, put her arms on her hips, and she narrowed her eyes to tell the man, "I don't believe you. If you don't tell me what I want to know, I'll call the police about you dealing in stolen goods. And don't think I won't!" Leona shook her finger at him to emphasize her impatience. Surely he wouldn't hurt her in front of the growing crowd. She waited for a response. Getting none, she continued. "What's it going to be?"

Behind her, Betty started softly saying, "Here, kitty, kitty. Here, kitty, kitty."

A few chuckles broke out through the crowd gathered around them. A baby fussed. A man coughed.

Beads of sweat broke out on Tattoo Man's upper lip. He looked nervously around at the crowd just outside his booth. "Keep your voice down. You're running off my customers." He looked around sheepishly at the gathered crowd and smiled. "Come on in and look around, folks. Nothing going on here but haggling." He waved his arms to welcome people in but got no takers.

He looked Leona square in the eye. "We don't take stolen goods if we know they're stolen. If anything here is stolen, whoever sold it to my uncle tricked him into thinking he owned it. It ain't my fault if my uncle got made a fool of." He pulled the blue bead necklace out of his pocket and flung it at her. She caught it as it started sliding down the front of her blouse. "That your necklace? Take it. You see your husband's wedding band? Take it. Whatever is yours, take it. Then get outta here, and don't ever come back!"

Leona quickly put the blue necklace and $20 into her purse and zipped it shut without taking her eyes off his face. She sensed nervousness, like he was the sidekick left holding the bag and the guilt. "First, tell me who gave these to your uncle."

Tattoo Man's knuckles whitened as he tightened his fists. The sweat on his upper lip spread to his forehead. He leaned toward her and whispered, "No. It's not good for business, if I tell who brings stuff to me and my uncle."

"The police will be bad for your business too. You can either tell me or tell them. You pick."

Tattoo Man tapped his fingers on the glass case as he held a debate with himself about what to do. He heaved a heavy sigh. "I think his name is T-Bone. He comes from the north end of Red Creek, up around Seventh Street. That's all I know! I've told you more than I should. Now go and leave me the—"

Betty jerked Leona's arm. "You got what you wanted. Let's go." She dragged her away from her stare-down contest with Tattoo Man with a quick pace. They rushed past Clarence who yelled after them to slow down.

Leona had the minivan going when Clarence finally got there, squeaking and puffing like an old steam engine. Betty filled him in on what happened as she helped him into the minivan.

"Don't even think it!" Clarence yelled at Leona as Betty put his walker in the back of the minivan. "We're not going on the north side. That's the bad part of town!"

Leona looked over her shoulder at him. "I didn't say anything about that."

"I know you. That's where you intend to go. Call the police and let them take care of it. Call that detective guy. You've done enough investigating on your own."

"I'm only just beginning." Leona set her jaw as she drove away.

CHAPTER 8

On the way out of the large parking lot, Clarence continued to object to visiting the north side of Red Creek. "Good people don't go there." When Leona refused to give in, he whined that he felt like a hostage being kidnapped. The silent treatment ended the argument as they headed north.

Clarence's pursed lips moved with his silent protests. Betty looked out her side of the minivan at the passing landscape, not saying a word.

Silence was golden and greatly valued by Leona. She didn't like making Clarence or Betty do something they didn't want to do but going to the north side alone seemed risky. Not that either one could help if trouble stirred up, but their presence would give her courage. Nothing, not even whiny companions, would keep her from her task.

She had a lead to follow and was determined to do it. She'd eventually tell Smythe about it so he could add it to the pile on his desk, but she'd go after this tip while it was hot. She chuckled to herself. Now she knew why Jessica Fletcher got such a thrill in solving crimes.

As they reached Red Creek's city limits, she wondered what to do if she found this T-Bone character. She'd never confronted a thug before—at least, she assumed that was what he was. The only hooligans she had met were students at her elementary school. An adult one would be hard to handle. How would she defend herself if he attacked? He might if he knew she suspected him of burglarizing her home. Was he the burglar or was it someone else? How would she find out for sure? She had no practice in interrogation. Maybe she should watch more of the modern crime shows to learn how.

She gripped the steering wheel even harder as the thoughts roiled through her mind. Joe always said to have a plan. But how could she prepare for something she had never experienced? There were too many variables, and likely even more than she could imagine.

Her best strategy was to stay cool and calm and sensible. She couldn't let T-Bone know how she found out his name. As much as she didn't like Tattoo Man, she didn't wish him any harm.

As she turned the minivan down Seventh Street, dread filled her. The neighborhood stood in stark contrast to her mature, well-established neighborhood. The houses here were old, small, from another era. Most were ill-kept and badly in need of repairs. The yards were either covered in dirt or the weeds were knee-high so that it looked like a jungle. Rusted cars and bits and pieces of toys lay beside the houses or in the yards. The trash-strewn gutters and neighborhood screamed out in neglect.

Maybe Clarence was right. Coming was a bad idea. This side of town had a dark feel to it. Joe always told her to stay away from this district because ninety percent of all the crime in town was in this area. What would he say to her now, driving down this street on a late Saturday afternoon looking for his wedding ring? He would be furious with her and tell her to let it go.

But she couldn't.

The visible poverty of the surroundings ended the silent treatment pact in the minivan when Betty contemplated out loud. "What kind of people name their son after meat? Seems like a silly name to me."

"It's probably a nickname." Leona weaved around the potholes that riddled the street while keeping an eye out for people. So far, they'd seen no one. The place seemed to be deserted.

"This is a bad idea!" Clarence repeated from the backseat. "And don't even think of shushing me. Joe would agree with me. You should call Smythe and tell him about this T-Bone character and let him handle it."

"I will after we find him." Leona slowed a little when they met the first car they'd seen since they turned.

Clarence let out a grunt of disapproval. "What are we going to do when we find him? Walk up and say, 'Did you rob my house? Can I get my stuff back from you?'"

"I won't accuse him of anything. I'm just going to ask him if he can help me find the ring and necklace and no questions asked." Leona tried not to shout. She took a deep breath to calm her pounding heart. "That's it. That's all I'm going to do. I even brought $20 to give him for his trouble."

"And I brought chocolate chip cookies." Betty picked up her huge bag and pulled out a small tin. "Two dozen. No one can resist chocolate chip cookies."

Clarence snorted. "I thought you were going to pay $200."

"I didn't get by the bank. It's all I have with me."

A smile spread across Betty's face. "My cookies will more than make up the difference."

"I'm sure a bad guy will change his life for $20 and one of Betty's cookies." Clarence's voice dripped with sarcasm. "And how are you going to find him? Start knocking on doors? How do you know he'll even tell you who he is? And how do you know that he'll even talk to you? What if he robs you again?"

"Tempt him with my cookies first." Betty shook the tin slightly.

Clarence let out a low growl like a lion in the bush. "I still say call Smythe first and ask questions later. Let him do his job and stay out of his way. We're out of our league!"

Leona shook her head but inside, she knew he was right. They had nothing with which to defend themselves in this hostile territory. The thought of the pawnshop owner telling her she needed a gun kept returning. Deep in her heart, she knew she could never use it to hurt someone else.

She turned a corner and saw a group of teenagers standing on the sidewalk. Most of them ignored the minivan driving by while two of them stared so intently that it made the hair on the back of her neck stand on end.

On the other hand, maybe having a gun wasn't such a bad idea.

A shot of adrenaline flashed through her heart, making it flutter. *What am I thinking? I would never fire a gun at anybody, especially young folks. I must be losing my mind to even think about it!*

Up ahead, Leona saw three people standing on the steps of a dilapidated house. The screen material on the door was hanging down and the front window had cardboard where glass used to be. An expensive, newer car sat beside the house, looking completely out of place. The two men and the woman looked to be in their twenties. They seemed to be talking lightheartedly, punching each other on the arms, laughing, and passing around a brown paper bag. Just friends hanging out. One of the young men put his arm around the woman and pulled her close.

"Maybe they know T-Bone." Leona slowed the minivan. She pulled to the curb on the opposite side of the street and stopped. The maneuver interrupted the young people's conversation and they all looked at the vehicle. They stared as Leona rolled her window down. "Excuse me, can you help me?"

They looked at each other. The tall skinny young man sauntered over toward the minivan. He stopped about twenty feet away and put his hands into the pockets of his faded hoodie that matched the rest of his tattered attire. The young man bent to look inside the minivan with a slight smile and a swagger to his stance.

The other young man and the girl came up behind him. The few clothes the girl had on were very tight, outlining her slim body. The young man with his arm around her waist looked like he fell off a GQ magazine cover. Judging from the dress suit he wore, the car belonged to him.

Hoody Guy spoke first. "You lost? The old folks' home is back the other way." He grinned and turned to share his derision with his companions. They joined in with his laughter.

Leona gritted her teeth, then relaxed her jaw. She forced what she hoped was a warm smile. "We're looking for someone named T-Bone. Have you ever heard of him?"

The people looked at each other and snickered. "What business you got with him, lady?"

Clarence stirred in the backseat. "They don't know him, let's get out of here!"

Not done with her interrogations, Leona kept her foot on the brake. "We want to ask him a couple of questions, that's all. Then we'll be on our way. We don't want to cause trouble."

Hoody Guy leaned down and looked inside again. "I don't know you or why you're here, but you need to turn this bus around and go on home before trouble finds you."

Betty leaned over, "Do you like cookies?" She held out her tin and rattled it a little. Pulling the lid off, she showed them her neat little stacks of sugary delights. She passed them to Leona who held the tin out the window.

Hoody Guy walked closer and leaned against the car, with the couple not far behind him. He eyed the offered tin suspiciously. "Sumpin' wrong with those cookies? Are they—*edibles*?"

Betty looked surprised. "Of course they're edible! They're delicious! I make the best cookies in South Dakota. Maybe the world!"

The man gingerly took the tin and pulled it outside. He took a cookie and bit a small piece off. A smile spread over his face as he held out the tin to his two companions. They each took a cookie to taste, then took several more of them. Suit Guy took most of the girl's cookies from her, telling her she'd get fat if she ate them. Hoody Guy quickly stuffed another cookie into his mouth.

Betty smirked at Leona and Clarence. "I knew you'd like them! Can you tell us where T-Bone lives? We need to ask him about some things that were taken from our house."

Leona quickly shushed Betty. "We weren't going to say anything about that," she whispered. Turning back to the window, she watched the young people eating and laughing with each other about something she didn't understand. When they started walking away, she leaned out the window and called after them, "You didn't tell us where to find T-Bone."

"Why you need to find him?" Hoody Guy asked with his cheeks stuffed with cookies. He stuffed his mouth with another cookie and threw the tin into the yard.

Betty started to get out, but Clarence grabbed her shoulders and told her to stay inside the minivan. Leona locked the car doors and hoped the three young people hadn't heard the deafening click. She squeezed the steering wheel with an iron grip, resisting the urge to speed away.

Leona watched as Hoody Guy put his hands in his pockets. Visions of guns flashed across her mind, causing her heart to beat even faster. She held her hands out the window so they could see she was unarmed. "I have a few questions that I hope he can help us with. That's all we want. Then we'll leave, and you won't see us again."

"Never heard of him." The young woman laughed as she looked at Suit Man. "Go home. You don't belong around here."

"Yes, we should go," Clarence urged in a loud voice.

"I want my cookie tin back," Betty whispered loudly.

"I'll buy you a new one." Clarence held onto her arm. "Stay in the car!"

Leona's last frazzled nerve gave way. "Please! I'm looking for my mother's necklace and my late husband's wedding ring stolen from our house. That's all I want. Nothing else. No questions. No police. Please help me!"

Hoody Guy stopped and turned to face the minivan. Rich Guy came up beside him and stood in a wide stance with crossed arms. An evil grin came across the face of Hoody Guy. He lifted his hand in a gesture that made Leona's face redden.

Leona let her foot relax on the brake and the minivan started to slowly move away. "Thanks anyway." Moving slowly away, the trio in the minivan watched the young people as they pointed and laughed at them leaving the scene.

Leona went to the end of the block and turned the corner to get out of sight of the rude behavior. "That went well. They thought we were idiots. And they're right."

Betty gasped and slapped her knee. "We forgot about the reward money. Maybe you should have offered them the $20 for information."

Clarence shouted an emphatic "NO!" so loudly that it choked him. After his spate of coughing, he croaked, "They'd have wanted more. And they might have robbed us. Don't bring money into the offer unless you want to lose that too."

A sigh of resignation escaped Leona's lips. She was at a dead end in her investigation. How was she going to find this T-Bone character in a neighborhood like this? Clarence was right. The offer of money would have made the situation worse. Moreover, what would she have done if one of them had been T-Bone? She shook her head very slightly. Forget her mother's necklace. It didn't really matter all that much anymore. Her heart ached to have Joe's ring back. To see it on his pillow once again, so she could feel he was close by.

Clarence was right about something else. It was time to go to Smythe and tell him what she'd found out. Maybe this information would spur him to action.

She guided the minivan along the street, crawling at a snail's pace, checking her rearview mirror to make sure they were not being followed by Hoody Guy and Suit Man. On this street, a few of the yards looked like some attempt was made to keep them neat and litter free, but the houses had the same dilapidated appearance as the rest of the neighborhood.

Betty pointed ahead. "What about asking those boys? They don't look nearly as intimidating as that last group who threw away my cookies and the tin."

Leona followed Betty's pointing finger to see a group of three boys, stair-stepped in age with the oldest looking to be about eight or nine years old. The oldest boy herded the other two along the cracked and buckled sidewalk. Their dark, long, unkempt hair matched their faded ill-fitting clothes. The two oldest boys wore shoes, but the youngest one was bare footed.

"You should have saved your cookies for them," Clarence told Betty.

Betty reached into her bag and pulled out another small tin. "I always carry spares." She let out a chuckle as she pried the lid off.

Leona pulled the minivan to the curb beside the boys and stopped. The oldest boy pulled the other two into the nearest yard and shielded them with his thin body. Large brown eyes watched Betty as she rolled her window down.

"Don't be afraid." Betty's voice was soft and grandmotherly like the woman in the gingerbread house might have talked to Hansel and Gretel. "We just want to ask you a question. And I have cookies if you'd like some." She held the container out the window.

The oldest boy stood on his toes to look inside the tin, but he stayed away from the minivan. He licked his lips as he held on tight to the younger boys.

"We are looking for someone named T-Bone. You ever heard of him?"

The youngest boy's face brightened. "T-Bone! He's..." The oldest boy put his hand over the young boy's mouth and told him to shut up.

"We don't know nobody named T-Bone. Why you wanna know?" The older boy let go of the boy's mouth and gently pushed him along in front of him as they continued down the street.

"No cookies then." Betty pulled the tin back inside. The youngest boy let out a moan of disappointment. The oldest boy pushed him along. Leona let the minivan creep along with the boys.

The boys stopped and stood in a dirt-covered yard. The littlest one looked up at the tallest one. "I'm hungry. I want some cookies."

Before the oldest boy could say yes or no, the middle boy ran to the minivan with his hand out. Betty kept the tin inside the vehicle out of reach. "You didn't answer my question. Do you know someone named T-Bone?"

The boy nodded and Betty handed him a cookie which he bit into eagerly. The youngest boy ran over. "I know him too!" Betty handed him a cookie. He stuffed it in his mouth and reached for another. Betty gave him one.

The eldest boy came over and held his hand out. Betty filled it with a cookie. "Can you tell us where we can find him?"

The boys stood with outreached hands and cookie-filled mouths, unable to talk coherently. The sight made Leona smile, although she felt a twinge of guilt for feeding hungry boys empty calories instead of something nutritious.

Clarence opened his door of the minivan. The boys watched wide-eyed as the automatic door opened without human help. "Hello! What are your names?"

The oldest boy took a big swallow. "I'm Doran. This here's my brother, Jaden and that's Tiger. What's your name?"

"Nice to meet you, Doran. I'm Clarence. The cookie lady is Betty, and our chauffeur is Leona." The ladies waved and smiled at the boys as they continued eating.

Betty rattled the remaining cookies in the tin. "Just a few left. You can have them if you answer one question. Do you know where we can find T-Bone?"

"Right here." A deep voice came from behind the minivan. Leona looked in the rearview mirror and saw Hoody Guy and Suit Man from around the corner, along with a very large man in a muscle shirt who looked even less friendly than the other two. The three of them had their tattooed arms crossed and stood with their feet wide apart, ready for a fight.

CHAPTER 9

Doran gathered the other two boys in his arms and pulled them away from the minivan. "We didn't tell them nothin'. We was only eatin' their cookies. That's all!"

Hoody Guy ran and grabbed the boys, slapping at them as he tried to hold them. The sound of blows filled the air, and Doran cried out in pain.

Unable to believe her eyes, Doran's scream shocked Leona out of her stupor. She threw the van into park and got out shouting, "Those boys didn't say anything. Leave them alone."

Clarence got out, hanging onto the minivan for support. "You stop that! Don't you hurt those boys!" He let go and wobbled. Leona was afraid he would fall, but he steadied himself with widespread arms. The damaged bone and muscles in his leg wouldn't let him go much farther. "Leave them alone!" he yelled as loudly as he could.

"Run!" Doran screamed out as he rolled away from the kicking feet of Hoody Guy. The young boys took off, with Suit Man and the big guy close behind them.

She ran toward Doran and pushed Hoody Guy away while she helped the boy out of the dirt. She pointed him toward the minivan where Betty waved for him to come.

Leona stood her ground. "I need T-Bone's help to find my husband's ring taken from my house." The big man came up holding the two smallest boys off the ground by their arms. He threw them at Leona's feet.

Suit Man had a scowl on his face. "You callin' me a thief? You gotta lot of nerve, granny!" He squared off at her. His fists were clenched, and he stood ready to move.

The two smallest boys got up and threw their arms around Leona's legs, with eyes as big as saucers. She huddled over them until she heard Betty call them to her. "Go to Grandma Betty," she whispered.

The boys ran to Betty's open arms. Clarence edged his way along the van and helped her pull them inside.

Leona's heart was beating so loudly she could hardly hear herself think as she stared at Suit Man. "I'm not calling you a thief. Someone—I don't know who—robbed our house and took some things that are very precious to me. I got a tip that you might be able to help me get them back. Please, if you can, help me find my dead husband's wedding ring and my mother's necklace. That's it. Nothing else. No accusations, questions, or police."

"A tip? Someone gave you a tip that I might have your junk? Who's the rat?" He came up close and shoved Leona.

She stumbled backwards, but she managed to keep her balance. The move left her discombobulated for a few seconds.

"Look, all I want to know is..." She took a deep breath and it seemed to clear her head. She stepped farther away from her vehicle to keep them away from the boys, Clarence, and Betty. "...can you help me find my husband's wedding band?" Her voice broke as she struggled to maintain control. "He died two years ago, and it's all I have left of him. I desperately want it back. The thief can have everything else. I just want my husband's ring. Please. Have a heart!"

"That's the truth!" Betty got out of the car. "Don't you hurt my sister!" She walked toward T-Bone. Hoody Guy stepped around T-Bone and pushed Betty backward so hard that she fell. She lay motionless on the hard-packed ground. Hoody Guy stood over her as if daring her to rise.

"Betty!" Leona screamed as she rushed toward her inert sister and knelt. Betty's eyes were closed, but she was breathing.

Clarence faltered and limped his way toward the prostrate women. He was barely standing but held his fists up as if they were threatening. "I'm a Vietnam war veteran! I'm not afraid to fight!" He swayed as he held his fists up and glared at Hoody Guy.

Adrenaline surged through Leona like spinach through Popeye. She jumped up, stood firmly in front of Hoody Guy, and shoved him away from Betty and Clarence.

With the ferocity of a lion, the young man came back at her and shoved her hard. She fell beside Betty and felt her head hit the hard ground. It stunned her and made her senses freeze in place.

T-Bone walked over, knelt, and grabbed the front of Leona's blouse. He pulled her up close to his face. "Get outta my hood before you really get hurt!" His foul breath circled in front of her face.

The fight hadn't left Leona. She rammed his knees with her fists which made him lose his balance and watched as dirt covered his fancy coat when he hit the ground. The man let out a grunt and scrambled back to his feet.

"Let me take care of her." The big man pounded his fist into the palm of his other hand.

T-Bone wiped the side of his mouth with his fist. "No, she's mine."

In a split second, she was standing, holding her fists in front of her. She didn't know how she got up so fast, and it left her dizzy. Even though she couldn't box or fight, if the former Marine Clarence could do it, she could too.

"What's goin' on here?" A woman's voice rang out. "What you doin' in my yard?"

"Nothin'," T-Bone called out over his shoulder. "Go back into your house, Miz Molly."

"Is that you, Terrance?" A big-boned woman came up behind him and stared at Leona and the others. Tall and stout, she looked as powerful and as threatening as an elephant matriarch defending her family. Her faded floral muumuu and flipflops added to her aura as queen of the jungle.

"Don't call me that!" T-Bone hissed at her. "Now git back in your house. Me and Jay is talking with these people."

In the distance, a siren was dimly heard. Leona saw fright flash in T-Bone's eyes before it was replaced by anger. T-Bone took a step toward her with a raised fist.

Leona braced herself. "Clarence, try to get Betty awake and back in the van." She never took her eyes off T-Bone as his compadres gathered around him.

The woman came between Leona and T-Bone. With her back to Leona, she mocked the young men. "Such a big man, Terrance. Pushing around kids and old people! You're real tough, aren't you." She pushed him, making him take a step back. His buddies stepped back as well. "You're just a bunch of bullies!" She pointed to Betty who lay still on the ground. "If you've hurt her, I'll press charges if they don't—" she motioned toward Leona, "—and let the police deal with you."

The woman grabbed the upper arms of Hoody Guy and the large man and took them to the other side of the minivan. "You're not allowed on my side of the street! Go back to your side and don't cross it again!" She heaved them toward the other side. They stumbled a few steps before regaining their swaggers.

T-Bone came up beside Leona. He reached inside his jacket. For an instant, she'd thought he was going to shoot her. When he pulled his hand out again, it was empty. He opened his mouth to say something, but he restrained his tongue. He straightened his collar and strutted across the street behind his boys.

When they reached the other side, T-Bone swirled around and pointed at the woman. "You keep those crazies on your side of the street. And you, lady..." He pointed at Leona. "Don't ever come around accusing me of being a thief. I won't be so kind to you next time!" With a flurry of foul language and rude gestures, the three men strode down the street before disappearing behind a house.

Leona got down beside Betty and checked for a pulse. A soft thumping gave the answer she hoped for. Betty moaned a little when Leona patted her cheek. "Betty, dear, can you open your eyes? Betty, please say something."

The woman leaned over Betty and looked at her. "Is she dead?" The boys joined her in looking down on the prostrate woman.

"Here, kitty, kitty," Betty murmured, opening one eye and fighting a smile.

"Oh, you stinker!" Leona gave her sister a love slap on the arm while the large woman gaped at the two women.

Betty moved to sit up. "Scared you, didn't I?" She giggled. "I figured if they thought I was dead, they'd leave us alone. Must have worked."

Leona let out an exasperated sigh of relief. "You scared the living daylights out of me. I thought for sure they'd broken your hip or worse."

The woman extended her hand to Betty. "You're lucky it's not. Looked like you landed hard."

"I'll certainly have a bruise, but no bones seem to be broken. All those years of drinking milk from Papa's cows paid off." Betty took the large woman's hand and after two attempts, managed to rise to her feet.

"I think I scared them off," Clarence called out from beside the minivan. "I must've looked pretty formidable to them." He laughed as he inched his way back to his seat.

The boys helped the woman get Betty back to the van and into her seat.

Leona looked at the boys and could see bruises starting to form where the men had hit them. Doran had a little blood coming from his nose, and Tiger was rubbing his shoulder. "Are you hurt? Betty, hand me one of those tissues."

"Naw, we're used to it." Doran wiped his nose on a tissue.

Betty cried out. "Used to it? No child should get used to that kind of treatment! It's abuse!"

Doran shook his head without saying anything.

Tiger looked at Betty with puppy eyes. "Got more of them cookies?"

Betty handed the tin to the boys. "You've earned them!"

The large woman leaned against the minivan. "Who are you? What are you doing here? If I hadn't heard you yelling, you could have been hurt pretty bad. Terrance and his gang ain't no kind of people to fool around with."

"I'm Leona Walker, and the cookie lady is my sister, Betty Drummond. Our manly escort is Clarence Brown." Leona wiped her dusty hand on her slacks and held it out in friendship. "Thank you for coming to our rescue."

The large woman raised an eyebrow, then took her hand and shook it. "I'm Molly. Kids around these parts call me Miz Molly."

Molly pointed to the boys. "I guess you already know Doran, the protector who is eight..." She pointed to the middle boy, "...Jaden, six, the one who gets into trouble all the time..." Jaden gave a squinty smile as he stuffed another cookie into his mouth. "...and Tiger, the quiet four-year-old who watches everything you do. They spend a lot of time over here."

Leona, Clarence, and Betty shook the boys' hands and thanked them for their assistance and apologized for getting them into trouble with T-Bone. Betty found another small bag of cookies in her purse and gave it to the boys.

"I thought they were yours."

Molly put her finger across her lips. "Boys, why don't you go inside and watch TV with Kendra and Zilo. Give them each a cookie please. You can play with them a while." The boys ran into the ramshackle house with a bang of the screenless screen door.

Betty asked, "You're not their mother?"

Molly shook her head. "Doran and Jaden's mother lives down the street. Tiger is their cousin. His parents are caught up in gang life, so they dumped him on Doran's mom. She's no good either. She's drunk or high most of the time, and she sells herself for extra money. How those boys have stayed sweet souls, I'll never understand. They need a loving home, but I can't give it. I'm raising my grandkids, and I ain't got room for more."

A lump made its presence felt in Leona's throat, and her eyes got misty. She knew they were good boys without being told. Living in that kind of environment, it seemed miraculous they were as gentil as they seemed. "Is there anything we can do to help?"

Molly's eyebrows shot up, then they came back down as she shook her head. "Get 'em a new home, I guess, but that ain't gonna happen. Y'all need to go back to where you came from and not come back to this side of town. What business made you come here in the first place?"

Betty waved her hand to get everyone's attention. "You won't believe our story. It started the day Al Watson saved our lives."

CHAPTER 10

The next morning, Leona, Betty, Clarence, and the three boys stood in the police station lobby while Smythe listened to their incredible story. Molly had allowed the boys to come with them on the condition they told their story about the confrontation if they left her out of it. If the boys' mother came looking for them, she'd make some excuse for their absence.

Betty and Clarence had argued over who would relate the facts of the event of the previous day. Clarence's version of the story about the face-off was all about how being a War veteran scared the scallywags off. Betty wanted to tell about how her cookies had saved the day.

Leona overruled them. She told Smythe about what had transpired between her and Tattoo Man at the flea market and later with them and T-Bone and his crew.

"I told you to stay out of it!" Detective Smythe rubbed his eyes. "We—not you" he wagged his index finger in her face "—are investigating. You're going to mess it up if you don't quit poking your noses into things you don't know anything about." He paced around the reception area, running his hand through his hair. "Who are these kids? Why are they here?"

111

"They're our witnesses." Leona stood beside the bench where Doran, Jaden, and Tiger sat. "We thought you might want to ask them questions."

Betty sat beside the boys with her arm across the back of the bench. "We offered to take them to McDonalds if they helped us out. You agreed, right, boys?"

Big smiles spread across their faces as they nodded.

Detective Smythe glared at the three and continued pacing. "You're telling me you bribed these boys to say whatever you told them to say. Do the parents of these kids know you've taken them? The lure of food is one of the ruses child molesters use to steal kids."

The elderly trio gasped and talked at the same time, denying such an intention. The boys fidgeted as the adults argued.

Detective Smythe gave a one-sided smile. "I know, but technically, I could make a case against you."

"We didn't kidnap them! They came willingly and with permission." While not exactly the whole truth, it was close enough. Molly knew they were here. "And not because we have any evil intent. On the contrary, we'd like to help these boys as much as we can." She took a moment to calm herself. "Look, we discovered valuable information we thought you should know. I told you about the man at the flea market and how he might have gotten my necklace from someone named T-Bone. We found out that T-Bone's gang lives in a house on 7th Street. Why can't you raid it? I bet there's all kinds of loot in there."

He pinched the bridge of his nose as he made a face behind his hand. "You got nothing but hearsay from some kids you found on the street and promised food to in exchange for them telling the story you told them to tell. That's not enough for a warrant. What you've really done is let him know that we're on his trail. You've spooked him, and he'll be careful now. He'll back out of his activities for a while, until things settle down. You've managed to stretch this investigation out even longer."

Her legs shaking, Leona lowered herself to the bench as the boys squirmed beside her. Leona could feel the necklace and the ring slipping away for good. She put her hand to her trembling chin to keep it from pushing too many tears out.

Tiger got off the bench and came over to Leona. He looked up at her with his large pleading eyes. "Can we go to McDonalds now?"

Smythe gave them one last disgusted look before starting toward his office in the back. "I have to get back to work and somehow try to salvage the damage you've caused. Please. Stay home. Let us do our jobs." He left the room without another word.

Doran looked up at Leona with worried eyes. "Are we in trouble? Can we still go to McDonalds?"

Betty smiled at the boys. "The only one in trouble is Leona."

Leona's heart was in her stomach, and her shoulders felt very heavy with the weight of guilt. She couldn't remember why last night in the dark, it seemed a good idea to bring the boys to corroborate her story. Her good intentions had only inflamed Smythe. The madder he got, the less likely he was to help her. On

113

top of everything else, Carly would be asking why they weren't at church that morning.

Clarence pushed his walker back and forth. The wheel squeaked like an alarm saying it was time to leave.

Betty was the first to move toward the door. The boys followed close on her heels. Clarence pushed his walker along behind them.

"Why does your wheel squeak?" Jaden asked.

"It doesn't." Clarence mussed the boy's hair.

With herculean effort, Leona lifted her heavy burdens and followed the others outside.

CHAPTER 11

Leona slowed the minivan in front of a house that looked like it should be condemned. It looked more like a shed than a house. The yard was full of rocks and weeds surrounded by a broken wooden fence that had once been painted white. The tall grass around a rusty old car told the story of how long it had been parked there. An uneven sidewalk led to a deteriorating concrete step. The screen door hung at an angle in front of the faded entry door.

Leona turned off the engine. "This is where you live?"

"Yep," Jaden replied from the back row of the minivan.

She pushed the buttons to open the minivan's rear door and side door and the boys clamored out. They went to the back of the minivan where several bags of groceries sat. They each took a bag and with an excited clamor, went up the crumbling walkway. Leona followed quietly behind with the last load of groceries. The boys disappeared into the house, leaving Leona on the front step.

"Yoo hoo!" She peeked inside the door that was ajar. "I need to talk to the boys' mother to explain where they were."

The door swung open and startled Leona. A skinny boy, looking to be about 12 or 13, stood there with a cigarette hanging from his lips. "You the one that gave them boys some food?"

"Yes, it's in return for a favor they did for us earlier today. Who are you?"

The kid took the cigarette from his lips and tapped the ashes off the end as he looked Leona up and down. "I'm Snake, Tiger's brother. Why are you here?" He took a long drag and blew the smoke toward her.

Her stomach tightened as the image of this boy-man digging through her jewelry case flashed in her mind. His proximity to T-Bone and his gang, along with his display of contempt, gave her the gut feeling that he might be one of the vandals. Maybe she should mention this kid to Smythe. She inhaled a small breath. "Is their mother around?"

A half grin moved Snake's face as the young man sauntered to a worn and tattered sofa and pulled out his phone. "She's doing yard work out back."

Leona gingerly stepped inside the tiny and filthy room. The boy plopped onto the sofa to watch a blaring big screen TV sitting on a folding table, spewing obscenities and sexual innuendoes. Leona was horrified by the noise. Doran came back. "Mom can't see you now. Maybe some other day."

"Are you sure? I think it best that I explain things to her."

Jaden called from the back door. "I'll take you to see her." Doran protested, but Leona pushed past him. She went through a kitchen where dirty dishes covered the table and countertops.

The groceries they'd bought for the boys were piled on top of the mess on the table, and she placed the last one there as well. Likely nothing would ever be put away in the dirty cabinets which was probably for the best. It would be more sanitary if they were used straight from the sacks.

She went out the back door into a grassy area that looked like a hay pasture. To one side, a woman lay face up with her eyes closed. A line of drool ran from her mouth down the side of her head. Leona bent over to make sure she was still breathing. She was.

Leona stood and looked at Jaden. "I thought that young man said she was doing yard work?"

"That's what we call it when she's passed out."

"Is she like this often?"

"Not all the time, but a lot."

Leona shook her head. "No child should ever see this." She straightened up and put her arm around the boy's shoulders and took him back into the house.

"Okay, well, I guess I'll leave now." She turned to go. "Doran, you can tell your mother about what we did and have her call me if she has anything to say about it. Thank you for your help today. I hope you and your brothers will be okay."

"Thanks for the food. Would you take us to McDonalds again sometime?" He followed her to the door.

Snake added his own order. "Next time, bring me something too. I need more cigarettes."

Leona stepped outside. "Maybe. Someday. We may drop off more food from time to time but no cigarettes. You're too young to smoke and besides that, it's bad for you."

Snake let out an unintelligible word and went back inside.

Jaden pulled her away from the door. "I'd like more food! You don't have to bring me cigarettes." He flashed a huge grin. The boys stood in line to get their hugs, eager for them. Tiger got in line twice. These boys needed lots of hugging. As soon as she stepped outside, she heard Snake yell for the boys to bring him some food.

When Leona got back in the minivan, Betty and Clarence asked what she saw. Leona could hardly speak, the scene had so repulsed her. She shook her head at their questions and blinked away the tears as she drove home.

Leona left Betty and Clarence having coffee at the house while she went back to the police station. She had an unsettled feeling in the pit of her stomach that had kept her up all night. She had to settle the matter without further delay.

The desk sergeant was in his usual, suppressed mood, refusing to let her see Detective Smythe. She calmly sat on a bench, took out her cell phone, and called the number on Smythe's business card. He answered quickly.

"Detective Smythe, where are you?" Leona asked, sweet as sugar.

"I'm at work. Who is this?" Even with not knowing it was her, his tone of voice was irritated.

"This is Leona Walker. I need to talk to you, and the sergeant out here won't let me in. Can you tell him you're working on my burglary case, so he'll let me come in and speak with you?"

The man didn't answer for a moment. "What do you want, Leona." It wasn't a question.

His demanding tone didn't surprise her. "There is a new matter that I need to discuss with you. It won't take more than a few moments."

A heavy sigh came through the phone. "Two minutes tops." He hung up without saying another word. The next instant, the front desk phone rang, and the sergeant growled that Leona could go back. She tried hard not to smirk, although a slight one might have leaked out.

The detective was leaning against the wall in the hallway with his arms crossed. "What's so important?" he called out in a frosty tone as she made her way past several police officers.

This attitude was not her idea of being a good public servant. "I want to talk to you about those boys that we brought here."

He stood up and uncrossed his arms. "What about them?"

"I told you about those thugs threatening the boys. I'm worried about them. Can you send someone out occasionally to check on them? To make sure they're...okay?"

He leaned against the wall again. "Don't they have family who looks after them?"

"When we took them home, their mother was passed out in the backyard. She's in no condition to care. Can you do something to protect them from T-Bone?"

With a slight eye roll and a quiet groan, "You can inform Social Services that you're registering a complaint about the living conditions and let them take it from there. Maybe they'll be taken to a foster home somewhere. Is that all?"

"Maybe. As long as it's a really nice foster home. And the boys must stay together. That's most important."

The detective stood up. "Your two minutes are up. Good day." He abruptly turned on his heel and walked quickly down the hall.

"But I was going to tell you about their brother, Snake! I think he was one of the vandals!"

Smythe disappeared into a side door without looking her way. Leona stood in the hallway and wondered if she should go after him but decided he was in no mood to listen. There was no denying it. She didn't like him. He was arrogant and unhelpful. He obviously had no intention of finding her necklace and ring. Now he didn't seem the least bit interested in protecting the boys. Wasn't that what police did? Protect the helpless?

She was a regular, untrained citizen, but she'd found T-Bone and his gang and now Snake. All of them should be on his list of suspects. Surely that was enough to solve the burglary and haul them in for questioning, get them to crack, and tell what they'd done with Joe's ring. The answer was right there in front of Smythe's nose. Didn't he care?

"How did it go?" Betty was cleaning the kitchen and getting ready to bake more cookies when Leona arrived. "We've been worried."

Leona poured herself a cup of coffee and leaned against the countertop. "Not good."

Clarence was sitting at the dining table watching Betty work. He cleared his throat. "We've been talking, and we think that maybe we're getting in too deep. This is starting to get dangerous."

Betty took butter out of the refrigerator and turned to face her sister. "I had a hard time getting out of bed this morning. I'm so sore from yesterday I can hardly move." She rubbed her backside and giggled lightly.

Leona laid her purse on the cabinet. She knew what Betty meant. Getting out of bed had been more painful than usual for her too. Her shoulder and hip hurt as she limped to the bathroom. If it hadn't been for the two extra-strength pain-reliever pills she took, she doubted she would be functioning as well as she was.

She told the two what had happened when she saw Detective Smythe and how he ignored everything she said. "I don't like Smythe, but I don't know who else to go to. I couldn't sleep all night, thinking about those boys. They seemed so hungry, and the place was so dirty. It's a wonder they aren't ill."

Betty nodded. "They seemed healthy, but after seeing the way they dug into those cookies, I knew they were starving. They grabbed those cookies like they hadn't eaten for days. That's why I'm making more. Maybe we can run them by later."

Clarence stood up, the first indication of energy from him. "We can do better. Let's take them good healthy food. Let's call the coffee group and go help them out."

Leona held up her hand. "Wait. We've already taken food. From what I saw, their mother is in no shape to make sure they are fed. Snake would eat it all. Today we should take food to Molly, and maybe she could see that they ate properly. She's a much more caring person. She's the one we should help, and in turn she'll help the boys."

Betty let out a cry of glee. "Marvelous idea! Molly came to our rescue. We can return the good deed."

Leona made herself a glass of iced tea as Betty mixed ingredients together. At last, a sense of purpose had returned to her life. "Clarence, why don't you start the phone tree."

CHAPTER 12

After meeting at the Bluebird Coffee Shop the next morning, the coffee group left to go to the grocery store. An hour later, they parked in front of Molly's house with a boatload of cleaning supplies, food, and a few new household items.

Molly came outside and stood in front of her door. With her hands on her muumuu-covered hips and her bare feet spread across the width of the door, she made a formidable barrier.

"Why're you here? I thought I told you not to come back."

Betty put her hand on Molly's arm. "My dear, the day before yesterday you helped us out of an unpleasant situation. Today, we are here with our friends to return the favor and help you out with a few things." She held her cookie tin in one hand and a box of donuts in the other. "We brought some treats and food and a few items we thought you might need. We'd like to clean your house in return for rescuing us when T-Bone tried to kill us. The men will replace the screen on your front door if you'd like." She signaled for George to lift the materials up.

Molly cocked her head and looked out the sides of her narrowed eyes. "I didn't ask for charity. I take care of my own."

Leona stepped forward. "It's not charity. It's repayment to you for your kindness. And..." she looked at the ground, hoping the right words would come to her, "...to ask you to keep an eye on Doran, Jaden, and Tiger." A lump formed in her throat, and she tried to swallow it. A deep breath calmed her voice. "I'm very fond of those boys. It must be the teacher in me. They need someone to watch over them."

"But they don't live here."

"I know, but they need a haven from their mother when she's doing yardwork, and someone to guide them and teach them that they can have a better life. They seem to feel safe with you. I know it's presumptuous of me, but I want to help them but through you."

Molly's face softened a little, and she spoke with less of a growl. "That's nice of you, but I don't run a foster home. I got my hands full with my own grandkids. They can come over when it gets bad, but they can't stay here."

Leona's heart sank a little. "I don't mean to impose or cause problems, but knowing they don't have a place to go when things at home get out of hand makes me cringe inside. I know it seems strange for me to be so attached to them, but I am."

Molly narrowed her stance and surveyed the people in her yard. An uneasy quiet settled over the group as she eyed them. "You say you brought food?"

"Yes, we did!" Betty led the procession up the front step. And treats for your grandkids. What are their names?"

"Kendra and Zilo."

Leona introduced their friends to Molly as the women went in the front door. The men stayed outside and began measuring the screen material. Clarence stopped at the foot of the stairs to the porch, turned his walker around, and sat down.

Inside, a small girl named Kendra and a toddler boy named Zilo sat frozen on a stained, sagging sofa in front of a small TV. They watched wide-eyed as the army of strangers invaded their hovel. Zilo scrambled to sit in Kendra's lap, and his thumb went in his mouth.

The living room was so tiny that only Leona, Betty, Irene, and Carly could fit in there. Betty carried the bag of groceries into the kitchen and called to the children on the sofa to join her. They obeyed and shortly returned to their places on the sofa with a donut in each hand.

Molly directed the chaos and told Kendra to go get the boys after she finished her donuts. The other ladies put their cleaning supplies on the small table and the worn countertops. The floor under their feet sagged in places and creaked when they walked over the ancient linoleum.

Carly tiptoed in with her hand like a surgeon scrubbed for surgery. She quickly set her bag down and put a tissue over her mouth. "I've not been feeling well so I think I'll go out to the car. I don't want to make anyone else sick." Carly backed out of the kitchen and quickly left the house.

Even behind the tissue on her face, Leona could tell Carly's face was scrunched up in disgust. How rude! Leona exchanged glances with Irene and Betty. She bit her tongue to keep from saying things she didn't want Molly to hear. She'd release her ire on Carly later. She stomped her foot hard and felt the floor give a little. She shouldn't do that again, or she might knock a hole in the floor.

Frustrated with herself and Carly, she tugged at the edge of a package of sponges so hard that it flew open and threw sponges all over. She shut her eyes as she felt her face turn a deep red. Even without looking, she could feel the eyes of the other women on her.

"I'd like to do that to her too."

Leona opened her eyes to see Irene with a smirk on her face.

"She deserves a good neck wringing, that old sourpuss biddy." Betty laughed out loud as she bent down to pick up the sponges. The others joined in her laughter, even Molly.

Irene put the sponges back into the grocery sack. "Please don't mind Carly, Molly. She's a snob to everyone, including her friends."

Molly shrugged and held her head high. "I do my best to keep this place clean and fit for my grandkids. I make sure they go to school, and we go to church on Sundays. I wash their clothes and make them take baths. They're good kids even though they ain't dressed in fancy clothes and we don't live in a fancy house." She crossed her arms, as if daring anyone to challenge her.

"And you do a great job!" Betty walked over to the lady and wrapped her arms around her large frame. "Kendra and Zilo are very lucky to have a caring grandmother to see after them."

Leona wiped away a stray tear. "Let's get these things unpacked. We guessed about what to buy so if you don't want some of these things, we'll take them home. We're not trying to force anything on you. There's no charity in these bags. Only gifts from friends in return for your act of kindness." She pulled out cleaning wipes, toilet paper, paper towels, and cans of food.

Molly opened several kitchen cabinet doors that held a can of soup, three boxes of macaroni and cheese, a few plates and glasses, and one pan. "I thank you for that. I wish all my acts of kindness paid off this good." She let out a belly laugh, and the others joined in.

Irene picked up the toilet paper and left to go find the bathroom. After a few moments, she returned. "I noticed you have a bucket under the bathroom sink to catch the drips. I told George to bring in his plumber tools. Before he got into insurance, he was a plumber's helper and knows a lot about it. He can see if he can repair it so it's as good as new."

Miz Molly's eyes grew damp. "We'd like that. If he fixes it, I don't have to get onto my grandkids when they forget to empty the bucket. I'll find another chore for them to do. Gotta keep them busy and outta trouble. Could he look at the leak under the sink in here too?" She opened the bottom cabinet door to reveal another pail with standing water in it.

Irene left to talk to George. He followed her back carrying a large sack in one hand and a toolbox in the other. "Here's the bread. Where's that leak?"

Doran, Jaden, and Tiger came bouncing in the house behind Kendra, excited to see what was going on. Leona presented each one of them with donuts, along with more for Kendra and Zilo, which put big grins on their faces.

Kendra looked at them and went to her grandmother. "Grandma, T-Bone and his gang are across the street. They hollered at us, and we came back in."

Leona heard Molly suck in a breath. "Leona, y'all need to go now. T-Bone looks for trouble wherever he can find it, and he won't like you being here. Run home now. Scat!" She waved her large arms like she was shooing flies.

Betty stood fixed to the floor. "But we ordered pizza to be delivered later."

When the word 'pizza' was spoken, the kids started shouting the word and dancing with glee. Molly tried to calm them down, but the surprise had been revealed. She was hosting a pizza party.

George brought his toolbox into the kitchen. "Got the bathroom leak fixed. Just needed the seal replaced. You shouldn't have any trouble now but leave the bucket in place for a day or two to make sure I got it. If I didn't, I'll come back and put new pipes in. Irene said you have a leak under the sink?" He set his toolbox on the floor and opened the cabinet. "I need room to work so you women should go supervise the screen door repairs."

Molly fidgeted nervously. "How long's it gonna take?"

"Depends on what's wrong." George got onto the floor and looked under the sink.

Molly paced a little. "All right. Go ahead and fix it. I don't need trouble with T-Bone, but I need my sink fixed worse."

The women moved to the living room where the kids were watching TV. Molly rubbed her forehead as she looked out her front window. "T-Bone doesn't like this. He can cause trouble for me. And you." She looked at Leona with narrowed eyes. "He came to see me after you left yesterday. He don't like you, so you need to watch out. Stay on your side of town."

Leona's heart fluttered with fearful butterflies. From Molly's worried look, the warning was not given lightly, and it wasn't taken lightly. The last thing she wanted to do was put this woman and the kids in harm's way.

"When the pizza arrives, we'll pay for it and leave." Leona pulled a piece of paper out of her pants pocket. "Here's my phone number. If you need anything, any time, call me. I have no compunction about calling the police if you need them. That way T-Bone can't blame you for it."

Molly nodded and put the paper inside her dress in her bra. She, Irene, and Betty went outside to watch Nick cutting the screen mesh to size for the door. Clarence was talking about something, with an occasional comment about how Nick was doing things. Carly sat with her eyes glued on her phone in their Escapade. Across the street, T-Bone and his buddies were talking in their huddle, making gestures, and sporadically throwing out a degrading comment.

Leona was glad everyone was outside. She wanted to talk to Doran while she had the chance. She pulled the boy away from the

TV to ask for more information about T-Bone. He was reluctant at first to say anything, but once he started, the floodgates opened. T-Bone was the head of a gang that lived in that house where they'd first seen him. Hoody Guy was his brother, and together they claimed the neighborhood as their own. He, Molly, and Hannah, Molly's neighbor, had a truce. He stayed on his side of the street, and they stayed on theirs.

Where did T-Bone get his money? The boy didn't say but told her lately there'd been more activity at his house than usual. He didn't know why. He told them he minded his own business and that's all he knew.

Nick declared he was done in the kitchen and went outside to join the others. She thanked Doran and left the kids with the TV. Leona went out just in time to see a strange woman staggering down the street, followed by a confused looking man. Both had blood-shot eyes visible from a distance. She looked around and screamed out, "Who 'er you and what the..."

Unseen, Doran stood behind Leona and screamed out at the same time she was yelling, "Momma, watch your language!" He stepped around Leona and ran over to his raving mother. He tried to calm her, but she looked at him with unfocused eyes. She wavered on her feet, then let out a barrage of profanities that shook the trees.

The people on the porch covered their ears and uttered prayers out loud. The other kids came out of the house to see the commotion but stood near the door. Carly honked the horn and vigorously waved for Nick to come. George told Clarence to take

Betty and Irene to the cars as he picked up his tools. Nick stood by Leona, with his hand on her elbow, ready to guide her safely away.

Doran came running back to Leona and looked up at her with sad eyes. "Miz Leona, you go home now. We have to go home so Momma will be okay." He turned and yelled, "Come on, Tiger and Jaden. Momma's calling."

Leona had trouble catching her breath and tears stung her eyes. These poor boys! Her heart ached for them. "Why don't you come to my house until your mother calms down?"

"No, Miz Leona." Doran held his hands up like he was telling a dog to stay. "You're the reason she's mad. It's better not to make her madder than she is." He turned to go, pulling his brother and cousin behind him.

Seeing the quiet conversation, Molly walked up to join in. "Doran is right. Go. I'll talk to their mother and get her to let them stay. She'll listen to me."

Her feet felt rooted to the ground, ready to defend the precious boys. "Are you sure I can't talk to her? I can tell her..."

"No." Molly's tone left no room for argument. "Go before you attract any more trouble or attention from her or T-Bone."

Leona's heart sunk, but she knew it was the right thing to do. "We never meant to cause problems."

"I know, but you don't belong here. Go back to your side of town." Molly hung her head and turned to go back to her house.

Leona called out to the group, "Time to go! George, please leave money for the pizza."

George approached Molly with his wallet out. He handed her a $20 bill. "It's already paid for, but here's a tip for the delivery boy." Molly took it, staring at it like a hungry dog looks at a bone. He gave her another $20.

Leona touched her arm to draw her out of the spell. "Call me if you or the boys need anything." The coffee group got in their cars and left Molly and the kids standing in the yard while the boys' mother raged in the street.

T-Bone moved to the middle of the street and gestured at them as they drove away.

Leona couldn't hold back the tears as she drove. Her jaw muscles started to ache a little from working so hard. She would never forget those boys or Molly. She'd come back later to make sure they were okay. She could bring the Eldorado and wear a scarf so no one would know it was her. No one was going to keep her from helping the boys.

CHAPTER 13

At breakfast the next morning, Clarence sat in his usual spot eating with the sisters. He cleared his throat after a sip of coffee. "I've been thinking, things aren't going the way we thought they would. We're going to places where we've never been before, mixed with people who we normally would avoid, been roughed up, hurt, and picked up—"

Betty choked on her coffee. "I don't remember picking you up off the ground. And since when have you become a Vietnam vet? You were stationed in Germany during that war."

Clarence gave her a don't-interrupt-me glare. "We've been in parts of town that we normally avoid because they could be dangerous. We had to listen to the ravings of a foul woman."

Leona stopped him from going on. "We also met a very nice woman named Molly who is doing her best under hard circumstances to do what's right. What about that?"

He shot her a narrow-eyed glance and went on. "AND we've made no progress toward finding your things. I think it's an indication that we should back off and let the police handle it." He let out a deep sigh. "And I think you should resign yourself to the fact that Joe's ring is gone."

Betty put down her mug. "I agree with you, Clarence. I think we've bitten off more than we can swallow. Don't you agree, Leona?"

"No, I don't." Leona pushed her plate of fruit and toast away from her. "I feel blessed to have met Molly and the boys. I have no regrets about that."

"True," Betty said. "They are genuinely nice people. Molly was thrilled when George fixed her plumbing. They need us. Don't you agree, Clarence?"

"No." Clarence stared at his coffee, then raised his head to speak. "It's the violent part of town. Sure, good people live there, but I think we cause more trouble than good by being there. How can we help them when we're on T-Bone's hit list."

Betty's mouth dropped open at his last words. Leona knew she had to salvage what resolve was left. "I doubt he has a hit list. We annoy him, and he doesn't want us around. Or maybe he feels threatened by us. No matter. Other than taking the boys home, we'll stay far away from him." She stirred her coffee even though it didn't need it. "You might be right about one thing, Clarence. We're in over our heads. I'm going to see Tristan today."

"Tristan?" Betty asked. "How is that corporate lawyer going to help?"

Leona shuffled a few toast crumbs with her thumb. "Now that we know about T-Bone, it's obvious his gang is responsible. Since Smythe won't investigate him, I'll talk to Tristan and see if there's anything we can do about getting another investigator. You want to go too?"

Clarence shook his head as he grabbed his walker and headed toward the door. "I shouldn't even be involved with this. My house wasn't robbed. I'm going to take a nap." The door shut behind him.

Leona looked at Betty who was biting her lip. "A nap? We haven't been up that long."

Betty got up and took her dishes to the sink. "Leona, Clarence is right. Your investigation is getting too risky, and we're too old for this kind of drama. After getting pushed down and the episode with the boys' mother, I think we all need a day of rest, don't you?"

Leona pushed the last few bites of breakfast around on her plate, then got up and took her dishes to the sink. "You can, but not me. I need to ask Tristan whether I should file a report with the police about their mother and the living conditions. What kind of guarantee do I have that they'd stay together and go into a good foster home? If they get stuck in a lousy home or get separated, I haven't done them any favors. At least where they are now, they have each other and Molly."

Betty rinsed the dishes and put them in the dishwasher. "Those boys have really stolen your heart, haven't they." She smiled at Leona who smiled back at her. She took off her apron that covered her lilac sweat suit.

Leona put her dishes in the dishwasher and shut the door. "It's the teacher in me. I love children, and it breaks my heart to see them in that bad home situation. Yet, despite their circumstances, they're very nice boys. How do kind and loving kids like them stay that way with all the bad influences around them? I want to help them grow up to be fine young men."

Prissy rubbed against Betty's legs until she leaned down and picked her up. Snuggling the cat in her arms, Betty said, "I'm sure you will."

Later that day, Leona and Betty sat in Tristan's office, hoping for good news. Leona detailed their visits with T-Bone and Molly. His raised eyebrows and gaping mouth through the whole explanation made Leona wonder if he even believed her. She ended with the plight of the boys and asked what she should do.

He sat motionless for a full minute before sitting back in his chair to rock slightly and tap his fingertips together. Leona watched him closely. He seemed unable to sit still for more than a second. Something on him was always moving. His legs, his chair, his hands. He was like a perpetual motion toy. Leona resisted the urge to frown. She looked down at her hands so she wouldn't have to watch his fidgeting.

"I'm going to be brutally frank with you. I think you need to butt out."

Leona's mouth fell open. Her jaw moved up and down while her brain struggled to find words that expressed her disbelief.

Tristan didn't wait for her brain to sort the matter out. "Let's put this in perspective. Your house was robbed, and that in and of itself is a traumatic event. Your space was violated, and you lost items that you value. Your insurance repaired or replaced many of the things you lost, but there are sentimental items you want returned. Right so far?"

Leona nodded without saying a word.

Tristan continued. "In your search for these two items, you've been in less-than-safe places, you've been threatened, you've been accosted, you've been royally cursed at. Right?"

Again, she nodded, unable to contradict him.

"You've possibly put a nice grandmother in harm's way because her neighbors know she's working with you, and you are working with the police. Her safety and the safety of her grandchildren could be in jeopardy all because you want to find the two small items that mean a lot to you. Do I have that down right?"

Leona gulped and nodded her head.

Betty pointed to Leona. "She's the leader of our gang. Clarence and I just go along to make sure she's okay. So don't blame us."

Tristan frowned as he rocked in his chair. "I'm not blaming anyone. T-Bone's gang won't differentiate between Leona and you two. In their eyes, you're all together in this." He tapped his fingers together as he scanned their faces. "You asked for my advice, and I'm giving it. Let the police handle it."

Leona rolled her eyes. "You don't understand. Joe's ring means everything—"

"Enough to endanger other people?" Tristan leaned forward and stared long and hard at Leona. For once, he sat still, waiting for her response.

137

Leona hung her head and said softly, "I didn't intend for that to happen."

"But it has. From what you've said, if T-Bone gets irritated at any of his neighbors, he could make their lives miserable. Are you willing to bear that responsibility?"

Leona felt as low as a gnat's knees. As much as she hated to admit it, this young whippersnapper was right. Her attempt to be her own investigator was a miserable failure. If anyone got hurt due to her bumbling efforts, she'd never forgive herself.

Tristan rocked in his chair again. "I think you need to accept that the ring is gone. The necklace is gone. But you have your health, your memories, your house, and your friends, so you're still a very lucky woman."

She couldn't argue with that last point. The former? Her heart wasn't ready to let go of Joe's ring, she moved in a different direction. "Can I get someone else to work on the case? Smythe doesn't seem to care."

His eyes closed to conceal something, likely an eye roll. She couldn't see it, but she felt it.

He slightly rocked his chair with his elbows on the armrests. "It's a small police department. There may not be anyone else. The investigation is ongoing, and that will have to be enough."

"So that's that."

"Yes. I'm not sure what you expect me to be able to do."

Betty moved in her seat. "Do like Perry Mason does. He has an investigator, Paul Drake, to move things along. Don't you have someone like that who can go look around for clues?"

Tristan leaned back again. "No. I can barely afford my cousin to be a receptionist."

Betty slapped her chest and gasped. "But Paul Drake helped Perry Mason win in the courtroom. I thought all lawyers had private investigators."

Leona patted Betty on the arm to calm her. "Now, Betty, Perry Mason was a TV show, not a real person."

"But I'd think all lawyers would want to be like him! He won all his cases."

"Only on TV. Don't lose touch with reality. This is real. Perry Mason is not."

Betty gave her sister a don't-patronize-me look. "What about Matlock? You going to tell me he's not real either?"

This conversation was inane and needed to end. Leona rubbed her aching forehead and brought up her last agenda item. "What about the boys? Should I report their mother to the police? If they take the boys away from her, would they be kept together?"

Tristan tapped his chin. "I know nothing about how child protective services and foster homes work. Just guessing, I'd say they'd keep the brothers together, but I'm not sure about the cousin. You'll have to ask them about that."

Leona's shoulders slumped. Tristan was a big disappointment. She came here for answers but got nothing but more questions. The trip had been a waste of time and money. She hadn't seen the bill yet but when it came, she'd probably be horrified at it.

Betty took Leona's hand. "You've done all you can do. The ring is gone, sister. Give up the chase. We can ask the boys what they want to do."

Leona left her lawyer's office more discouraged than ever. "Go home," he'd advised her. "Let justice take its course." He promised to keep them informed about the investigation's progress and said he'd check with child protective services about their processes.

Betty didn't seem to mind going home without a way forward. She chatted cheerfully about nothing of consequence on the way, driving Leona to the edge of screaming.

Leona knew that she couldn't sit around and wait for something to happen. Almost two weeks had passed since the crime, and every passing moment pushed her farther away from finding Joe's ring. No, she wouldn't take Tristan's advice. She would cling to hope. She didn't care about justice. Justice was only interested in finding who did this and not in recovering the ring. It was up to her to do that.

CHAPTER 14

Betty was in the kitchen, baking and cooking. Clarence sat at the table watching her work. Their babbling was of no interest to Leona. She called Molly a couple of times to check on the boys. She was restless. To stay focused, she planned another foray to the flea market. Answers to her questions may be there if she could pry them out of Tattoo Man. He could tell her which gold dealer had Joe's ring. Once she found that out, she'd go there and hope that it was still a ring and not a blob of metal.

Friday morning dawned bright and warm, and Leona offered to take her companions out for breakfast. Never suspecting a thing, they accepted and came along for the ride. Once the meal was over, she revealed her true purpose.

"We're going back to the flea market. I want more of those delicious tomatoes. And I'm going back to talk to Tattoo Man. I think he knew more than he was saying, and I want to ask more questions."

"Have you lost your mind?" Clarence bellowed from the backseat. "I want to go home!"

Betty patted Leona's arm softly. "Now, Leona, you heard what Tristan said. Let's go home, and you'll feel better. Be patient."

141

"I've been patient! No more. I want Joe's ring back before it gets melted down, and time's a-wasting!"

The whole way to the flea market, Clarence continued to voice his disapproval of her mission and his desire to go home. He was being kidnapped against his will, he declared. Betty offered Clarence a cookie which silenced him for a few moments. She offered one to Leona, but when she refused, Betty stayed quiet, looking out the window without saying anything.

After Leona parked, she gathered her purse and turned to the others. "Who's going with me?"

Betty took a bag of cookies out of her tote, took hold of her cane, and opened her door to get out. Both ladies looked back at Clarence, who was frowning.

He crossed his arms. "I don't think you should go. It's a bad idea to go back to where you obviously weren't wanted the first time."

"Fine. Stay here." She put the keys on the center console in case Clarence needed them to roll the windows down or lock the van if he left to find a restroom.

"You'll be sorry. When he yells at you again. I won't be there to protect you."

"I'll be the one doing the yelling today. I'm fed up with the whole situation."

Clarence made no move but eyed the keys. "Maybe I'll just drive myself home."

Leona picked the keys up and put them in her purse. "Be back in a bit." Leona got out with Betty close behind.

The two ladies made their way through the maze of booths and customers, passing by the crate full of large, red tomatoes. Leona saw Tattoo Man talking with a customer as she walked up to the jewelry case. He looked her way and made a face. He took a step backward, and Leona was afraid he was going to run. When he picked up an item and showed it to his customers. Leona breathed a sigh of relief. She looked through his jewelry display and out of the corner of her eye, saw him frown. Nothing in the case looked familiar. Joe's ring still wasn't there, and neither was her mother's necklace nor any other piece of her stolen jewelry.

He came over and whispered out of the corner of his mouth, "I told you not to come back."

"I know. I'm just checking. Has anyone offered to sell you a gold band?" She took her mother's photo from her purse. "Or tried to sell you this necklace?"

Tattoo Man didn't even look at the photo. "No. Now go away."

"It's not good business to run customers off like that. Plus, it's rude." Tattoo Man, Betty, and Leona spun around to see Smythe and another man with a badge handing from his belt standing there. Smyth had a smug look on his face. He leaned against the glass cabinet. "Why don't you tell her the truth? That you saw her things and already sold them."

Tattoo Man's face paled, and his mouth fell open. He stuttered, looking for an excuse. Smythe held up his hand to silence him.

"I talked to the gold buyer downtown and found out that you sold him several gold wedding bands last week. It's likely her missing ring was one of them."

Leona felt like the earth was about to start spinning out of control. She grabbed the case to keep her balance. Betty reached out to steady her.

Smythe put his hands on his hips, pushing his suit jacket behind his hands. His shoulder holster and pistol were visible with his stance. "I'm sorry to tell you this way, Mrs. Walker, but your ring's been destroyed."

"I didn't know any of them was stolen." A sweat drop fell from Tattoo Man's red face. "People bring me their stuff and tell me it's theirs. How can I know if it was stolen? You can't arrest me for that!" He started to back away, but Charlie told him to stay where he was. Tattoo Man froze.

"You hear that, Leona?" Smythe turned toward her. "The ring is gone so you can stop looking for it. Understand? Go home. Grieve. Learn to live without it."

The words stabbed her heart. Her brain wouldn't work right, and she didn't know how to respond. Things swirled in her head. Anger. Confusion. Grief. Fear. Loathing. She gripped the case so tightly that it hurt her hand, and the pain brought her out of her trance.

"Thank you for your time, gentlemen." Betty took Leona by the shoulders. "I'll take my sister home now."

Leona steadied herself before letting go of the jewelry case.

Just then, a young woman walked in from the back. She went up to Tattoo Man and told him she'd finished unpacking the boxes. Leona stared at the woman's neck. Her mother's necklace hung around it.

"That's my mother's necklace!" Leona pointed at the girl. She dashed around the jewelry case as quickly as her legs would carry her. With outstretched hands, she lunged at the girl who screamed and shrunk back. Leona got her mother's photo out of her purse again and waved it around. "Smythe! That's my necklace! I have proof!"

The girl froze, her eyes wide. She looked to Tattoo Man, stepped behind him, and turned slightly like she was getting ready to run.

Smythe stepped between Leona and the girl. "Let me handle this. Young lady, where did you get that necklace?"

The young woman's demeanor changed in an instant. She put one hand on her hip and flipped her head back. "Who's this old lady? And what's she talking about? I got this necklace from my boyfriend. It's mine!"

"Your boyfriend's a thief! Arrest her, Detective!" Leona reached around Smythe for the necklace, but the girl agilely jumped away from her reach. She held her hand on the necklace, blocking it from Leona's view. She spun on her heels and ran out the back way. Leona tried to follow her, but Betty and the other policeman held her back.

"She's got my mother's necklace! Go get her!" Leona was writhing, trying to free herself from their grips. "Why aren't you chasing her?"

"Stop it!" Smythe held his hands up toward her. "Stop or I'll arrest you for impeding an officer!"

Leona stopped fighting him and looked around. Every eye in the building was on her, staring and wondering. Even Tattoo Man and Betty looked at her like she'd lost her mind. Maybe she had.

Charlie loosened his grip. He motioned for Tattoo Man to follow him, and they went out the way the girl had gone.

"I'm sorry." Leona straightened her blouse. "Why are you still standing here, Smythe? She's a suspect in the robbery of our home! Do your job!" Her voice was getting louder and more desperate.

Smythe got in her face. "I told you to leave this to me, but noooo. What do I have to do to keep you out of my business?" He pulled back, his face red as he looked around the gathered crowd.

"You could have found my Joe's ring before it was destroyed but you didn't." Her voice broke as she said the words. She pointed toward the back where the girl had disappeared. "That girl has my mother's necklace. It matches this photo that I showed you weeks ago. Yet here you stand letting her get away. Why don't you do your duty and catch her? Get my necklace and ring back. THEN I will leave you alone."

Smythe jabbed his finger at her face. "You don't know what you're dealing with! You need to back off before you get someone hurt!" Closing his eyes and tightening his jaw, he backed up and took a deep breath. "I don't want you to get hurt." He almost seemed sincere.

Betty quickly opened her purse and pulled out a cookie-filled bag. "Cookies anyone? Things always look better over cookies." It swung from her grip between the two enraged foes.

146

Smythe blinked, then grabbed the bag and sent it flying off into the crowd.

Betty let out a cry and went in search of her precious cookies.

His face redder than ever, Smythe opened his mouth to say something, but turned, walked through Tattoo Man's booth, and went out the back entrance, leaving Leona glaring after him.

Betty returned with cookies in hand. "Come on, Leona. Time to listen to Tristan and Smythe. There's nothing else here so let's go home."

"Yes, there is! Go get in the van with Clarence." Leona ran out the back way. Her mind told her to run, but her legs could only manage a fast trot. Too much time in her recliner and sewing chair had robbed her of the ability to move any faster.

Trucks and vans were parked in rows. The policeman, Tattoo Man, Smythe, and the girl were nowhere to be seen. She trotted along one row of vehicles looking between them and beyond them into the next row. After going the length of the parking lot, she stopped and leaned against the front of a big truck. Sucking in great gulps of air, her legs felt a little wobbly, but she pressed on at a slower pace.

An hour later, Leona gave up. Smythe and the girl had disappeared. Her feet hurt from running and walking around so long and being so out of shape. Her blouse was damp with perspiration. She limped slightly as she approached the minivan. The glares sent her way from Clarence and Betty caused her to stop in her tracks for an instant. It must be her punishment for dragging them along and making them wait. She got into the hostility-filled vehicle and hoped her sweat odor didn't make the situation worse.

On the drive home, little was said. Clarence fell asleep in the backseat. Betty rolled the side window down a bit and looked out. Leona fumed. Her mother's necklace had been so close, she could have grabbed it off that girl's neck if only she'd been quicker. If only she had chased that girl as soon as she left. If only Joe hadn't died.

The worst part was that the girl looked familiar, but she couldn't remember where she'd seen her. Somewhere unexpected and not too long ago. McDonald's? The grocery store? She racked her brain, but nothing useful came. She let out a soft growl, frustrated by her not-what-it-used-to-be memory.

Doran, Jaden, and Tiger were playing in her yard when they came down the street. Doran seemed enthralled with her rose bushes under the bedroom window but ran back to the porch ramp when he saw them coming. Jaden and Tiger were rolling around in the lush grass, oblivious to their arrival. When they saw the minivan turn into the driveway, they jumped up and ran to Doran. She stopped short of the garage and turned the motor off. The boys smiled and waved like a welcoming committee.

"What on earth?" Betty opened her door. "They're a long way from home." She called out to Clarence who woke from his nap.

He stirred, cleared his throat, and took off his seatbelt. "About time we got home. I need to find a new taxi driver." He got out and hung on to the minivan until Leona brought his walker. As she gave it to him, Leona pointed out that they had company.

He squeaked his way around the minivan to where the boys were standing. "How'd you get here?"

Tiger ran up to them. "We ran. We're good runners."

"You got a squeaky wheel." Jaden pointed at the offending part.

"Oh, so now you're an expert in fixing things?" Clarence raised his eyebrows. "I don't hear any squeak." He pushed his walker forward and backwards a bit. "This works just fine."

Tiger ran over to Leona and gave her a hug around her middle, followed by the other boys who expected hugs before moving to do the same to Betty. Leona was more than happy to give them but noticed Tiger's pants were a little too big. Someone had fashioned a belt out of rope which held them up. Most of their clothes belonged in a rag box. On their feet were shoes that should have been discarded long ago. A trip to the store to get new clothes and shoes was in order before taking them home. She could even get something for Kendra and Zilo.

Leona sat in her wicker chair as Betty went inside to get Prissy. The boys piled on the porch swing. "What are you doing here? How did you find out where I lived?"

Tiger shouted out, "We went to the liberry! Doran knows how to use the computer!"

"I know how to Google." Doran beamed with pride in his accomplishment. "You can get maps from it."

Clarence and Leona looked at each other. "Wow!" said Clarence. "That's impressive! You're a very smart boy, Doran."

The look on the boy's face after being paid a compliment caused Leona to tear up. Obviously, the boy didn't hear kind words often, and he absorbed them like a sponge. Leona hoped he'd cling to those words when his life was less calm.

Betty came outside with Prissy on her leash. The boys ran to the cat who retreated with an arched back. Betty picked her up and held her close as she stroked the hostile cat's head. "It takes her a while to get used to new people," she said. "You have to go slow and easy around her. Let her settle down, and she might let you pet her later."

"Or not," Leona said. "She still won't let me hold her. Boys, tell us why you're here."

"Our mother told us to come tell you that she's sorry for the way she acted when you were there last time," Doran said. "She liked that you bought food for us. She says that's real Christian of you."

"She wanted to call you, but we wanted to come see you," said Tiger.

"Does she know you're here?" Leona gave them a hard look.

Doran shrugged. "I dunno. We didn't tell her. She was busy."

Leona dug through her purse to find her cell phone. "How about we call her and tell her we'll bring you home." She gave her phone to Doran. If he could work a computer, he would have no trouble calling his mom on her phone.

"Miz Betty," Tiger said shyly. "You got cookies?"

Betty laughed. "Do I have cookies? Of course, I do! I'm the cookie lady! I'll get them, and we'll have a picnic on the porch." She took Prissy inside with her.

Leona watched the boys play on the porch swing. The boys had triggered a memory. She'd seen that girl on the front step of

T-Bone's house. She was the one hanging around him and Hoody Guy. Her chest felt lighter. When she took the boys home, she'd go by T-Bone's house to check on the girl and offer to buy the necklace back. She'd lost Joe's ring, but she wouldn't lose that necklace.

It was after suppertime when the boys marched into their kitchen clad in new clothes carrying three bags of groceries, smiling like they were carrying precious gifts of gold. The carpet looked a century old, worn and holey. The drabness and deteriorated interior were depressing to Leona. Her heart gave her a twinge of guilt for living so well while the boys lived in such dire conditions.

The boys' mother, Lila, seemed mostly sober as the boys showed her what they brought home. The slight trembling in her hands and her bloodshot eyes exposed her tenuous condition. She thanked Leona and Betty for the clothes and the extra food.

Jaden's smile lit up the room. "Mom! They gave us $20 each at the grocery store, and we got to buy whatever we wanted! Look what I bought!" He pulled two boxes of cereal, two big cans of spaghetti and three cans of chili.

"We planned it out," Doran said as he unloaded his hot dog buns, frankfurters, and lunch meat. He helped Tiger put both of his sacks on the table. Tiger climbed into a chair and pulled out milk, bread, and three bags of potato chips.

151

"No veggies in the mix," Betty said as she added baby carrots and large bag of cookies to the pile. "They didn't seem too interested in those."

"And look at our new shoes!" Tiger held up his foot, showing his brightly colored shoes that flashed each time he took a step. "Now I can run like the wind!" He ran around the small living room making wind sounds with his mouth.

Their mother gave a weak smile. She swayed slightly and her red eyes seemed to redden more. Jaden hugged her around her waist as she stroked his hair. Not making eye contact, she murmured, "Thanks for what you've done. I like seeing my boys happy. We have a hard life, but my boys are good kids."

"Yes, they are. I think the world of them." Leona wiped her eyes. "We should go now. Boys, eat well and be good!" She held out her arms, and they ran to her for a parting hug.

As they drove away, Leona turned the corner and stopped in front of T-Bone's house. "I finally remembered where I had seen that girl with Mother's necklace. She was with T-Bone that first day we came. I'm going to see if she's here. Maybe President Grant can persuade her to give it to me." She waved the $50 bill around before stuffing it in her pants pocket.

"Are you nuts, Leona?" Clarence said from the backseat. "There's no telling who or what is in that house. It could be very dangerous. I'm in no shape to come to your rescue." He pointed to the house. "If T-Bone is in there, he may put you out of your misery. I say we go home."

Betty joined in with Clarence, "He's right, dear. Maybe we should call Smythe and tell him about it."

"Smythe wouldn't do a thing. He didn't even chase that girl after we saw her. No, I'm not calling him." Leona opened her door. "I'm going in. You stay and call for help if something happens." She got out and walked around the minivan. She heard the minivan doors open and Betty clanging Clarence's walker around while trying to get it out. "I said stay here—"

"We're in this together, little sister." Betty helped Clarence with his noisy walker.

Perturbed yet grateful, Leona paused to let them catch up before she started up the crumbling sidewalk.

Clarence's squeaky wheel was like a car alarm, announcing their presence to the neighborhood. A dog barked nearby, and booming music beat its way down the street. They didn't see or hear anyone as they crept toward the door.

"I wonder if anyone is home?" Betty tucked in closer to Leona.

"What're you doing here?" A voice boomed out across the quiet neighborhood.

The sound sent bolts of fear through Leona. The trio jerked around to look behind them. There Molly stood like an angry mother ready to ground her kids for disobeying her.

Leona grabbed her chest to calm her racing heart. She waved her arm, hoping Molly could see it in the dim evening lights.

Molly waved at them to join her on the sidewalk. "What you up to?" She stood with her hands on her hips.

"Why don't you two go tell her I'm looking for that girl" Leona turned back toward the house.

Clarence cleared his throat. "Why don't you come ask her what she knows about the girl first."

There Clarence went again. Having a good idea she couldn't ignore. The three of them joined Molly, and Leona told her about the visit to the flea market, about seeing the girl with the necklace. "I want to offer to pay for my mother's necklace, so she'll let me have it. She might even know where I could look for Joe's ring."

A deep frown covered Molly's face as she looked up and down the street. "T-Bone and his hoods are gone right now. I haven't seen Janelle. I guess there may be a chance she didn't go with them."

"Want to come with me and see?" Leona gave her side glance.

Rubbing her face, Molly paused, then shook her head. "Girl, you're gonna find yourself in hot water, and you're gonna wish you'd never put a toe in. If you're crazy enough to insist upon going, I'll go and try to keep her from killing you."

As Leona and Molly went past Clarence, he muttered, "So now she's roped you into trouble too. You're both nuts. You have no business over there."

"Hush, Clarence. You and Betty stay here and keep an eye out for T-Bone."

"And do what? Go to war with them to keep them at bay?" Clarence let out a snort. "Come on, Betty, we'll get in the foxhole and watch the fireworks when they start."

Leona and Molly walked up the sidewalk, climbed the steps, and knocked at the door. It swung open by itself at the first knock to reveal a mostly empty room. The faded paint on the walls and the washed-out color of the shabby carpet emphasized the neglected state of the structure.

"Yoohoo Anyone home?" Leona waited but heard nothing in response. She took a step inside.

"Leona, get out of there!" Clarence yelled from the minivan. "You're breaking and entering."

Leona spun around and waved her arms at him, signaling for him to keep his voice down.

Miz Molly took Leona's elbow. "I think we should listen to Clarence."

"Leave if you want, but I'm not. The door swung open on its own. I won't go in very far. Just enough to see if anyone's home."

Leona stepped just inside the door and looked around the small living room that opened into a hallway. "Yoohoo!" She waited for an answer but heard nothing. She took another step inside. "I'm Leona Walker. I'm looking for the young lady that lives here. I want to buy that necklace she was wearing today at the flea market." No response. "No questions asked about where you got it." No response. "Is anyone here?"

"No one's home." Molly remained in the doorway. "Come on out of there, and let's go to my house."

Leona waved her off. The streetlights dimly lit the small room as she tiptoed across the living room and looked into the kitchen. Seeing nothing, she turned around and crept back into the living room. In the dim lights, something in the hallway caught her eye. On the floor, a pair of legs stuck out of another room. Thinking about the boys' mother doing yard work, she went to see if the person needed help. As she got to the doorway, she could see inside. The girl she was looking for was lying there, lifeless eyes staring at the ceiling. Her mother's necklace was still around her neck.

CHAPTER 15

Blue and red emergency lights lit up the crowd gathered along the yellow crime-scene tape that encircled T-Bone's house. Police buzzed in and out like bees around a hive. Doran, Jaden, and Tiger stood behind the yellow tape, kept there by the vigilant eye of a policewoman after their many attempts to run into the house. Molly stood behind the crowd.

Inside a nearby police cruiser, Leona sat sideways on the seat with her feet on the ground. Betty sat in the minivan, and Clarence sat on his walker's seat at the back of the minivan where a policeman told him to stay.

Smythe came up to Leona and leaned on the open car door, shaking his head and tsking at her. He took a card out of his pocket. "You have the right to remain silent. Anything you say can and will—"

"You're arresting me?" She started squirming to get out of the car, but he yelled at her to remain seated in the car.

"Anything you say can and will be used against you in a court of law. You have the right to an attorney. If you cannot afford an attorney, one will be appointed for you. Do you understand the rights I have just read to you?"

157

Hot, angry tears burned her eyes. *Joe, I need your help to get out of this mess. Why did you leave me?*

Smythe repeated the question louder.

Leona nodded. She might have to take the appointed lawyer. Tristan would be no help with this.

"With these rights in mind, do you wish to speak to me?"

"I didn't kill her. I found her already dead and immediately called 911."

He ran his hand through his hair. "I'm not surprised to find you here with a dead body and your mother's necklace that was used to strangle her." He leaned down to get closer to Leona's face. "Just how bad did you want it back?"

Leona's mouth fell open, then her eyes narrowed in anger. She leaned forward so he would not mistake her answer. "Not bad enough to kill someone. I would never do that. And you know it!"

He straightened up. "Last time I saw you, you were running after her at the flea market. Did you follow her here and kill her because she wouldn't give the necklace back?"

Leona let out a harrumph. "Now you're being ridiculous! Of course not! I never saw her after she ran out. I tried to find her, but she outran you and me. I came here to see if she'd sell me the necklace." She reached into her pocket and pulled out the fifty-dollar bill. "See? I came to buy it from her. I'll say it again, I didn't kill the poor girl."

Smythe stared at her without moving a muscle for several minutes. Slowly, he stood upright, took out a notebook, and wrote in it.

She couldn't make out his expression because he had his back to the light.

"Where did you go after you left the flea market?"

She crossed her arms and looked the other way. "I spent the afternoon shopping. I have the receipts to prove it. And Molly can testify that the girl was dead when we got here."

He made more notes. "What did you do after you left the flea market?"

The question was repetitive to her, but maybe it had a purpose. "We went straight home and found three little boys who needed shoes and food. We came to this neighborhood to take the boys home. When I remembered where I'd seen the girl before now, we stopped so I could offer to buy the necklace from her. She was dead when we got here. I. Did. Not. Kill. Her!"

Still scribbling in his notebook, he asked, "How did you know she lived here?"

A shot of adrenaline flooded her body. Knowing she couldn't avoid it, she told the whole tale of how she followed the clue from Tattoo Man to this area and all the things that had transpired since then. Some of it she'd already told him, but she repeated it so he could write it in his notebook.

At the end of her story, he paused in his writing. "What're the names of the boys? Are they the ones you lured to the police station?"

Leona hesitated. "I'd rather not say. They're harmless kids that had nothing to do with any of this."

159

The veins on Smythe's neck started to bulge as he worked his jaw. He flexed his fists. He got so close to Leona's face that his breath ruffled her hair. "What were you really doing here? I want to know!" His voice echoed through the house.

Another man walked up next to Smythe and put his hand on his shoulder. Smythe straightened up. The two men walked away from where she sat and talked. The other man was the same one who had been at the flea market earlier with Smythe. He motioned for Molly to come over. Leona heard him say, "Molly, you're free to go home. Thanks for your help."

Molly left without saying a word or giving a look at anyone. Leona closed her eyes and said a prayer. *Don't let me be foolish enough to lose her as a friend. The boys need both of us.*

The man came back to her and pulled a badge from his coat pocket. "I'm Charlie Walters. Homicide and Major Crimes Division from Rapid City. You said you were in the neighborhood. Where did you go?"

The man seemed calm and professional. More like a policeman should act. Leona gave him the address.

"Why did you go there?"

"To take the three little boys home. They'd walked to my house, and we brought them back."

"How did you end up in here?"

Leona took a deep breath of exasperation. "I saw this girl—the one who is dead—earlier today at the flea market. You were there, remember? She had my mother's necklace on. The one stolen from my house a couple weeks ago. I'd seen her here with a guy named

160

T-Bone and some of his miscreant buddies. After dropping the boys off, I wanted to see if she'd sell my necklace to me. Molly came along to protect me from T-Bone if he happened to be here. Betty and Clarence are here because I dragged them along. They didn't want to come. That's the whole story, and that's the truth."

Smythe rushed over and leaned over to get in Leona's face again. "I think you're lying! You came here looking for T-Bone. You think he robbed your house and sold that gold ring you've been looking for. I told you it had been destroyed, and you got angry. Very angry. Angry enough to kill!"

Leona raised her volume so everyone could hear. "I. Did. Not. Kill. Her!"

The other cops and investigators stopped to see what was going on. Smythe remained inches from Leona's face as she returned his glare. The battle of wills was intense.

"Here, kitty, kitty."

Leona was startled by Betty's voice coming from behind Smythe, but didn't break her eye contact with the detective. The intensity between them eased infinitesimally while she tried to figure out what was going on.

"Here, kitty, kitty."

Leona was the first to look at Betty. Betty leaned on her cane, holding her hand out. "Here, kitty, kitty."

Everyone stared at her. She smiled sweetly and said, "You boys want some cookies? If you help me find my kitty, I'll let you have some."

Smythe looked at Leona with a question in his eyes. Leona shrugged. "She gets a little ditzy sometimes."

The tension lowered as the investigators chuckled before going about their business. Olivia Torrez guided Betty back to the minivan. Smythe stood back. Charlie stepped in front of him to talk to Leona. "We should talk to the boys you brought home. They might know what's been going on around here."

"Are these the same kids you bribed to corroborate your story about T-Bone attacking you?" Smythe's eyes narrowed as he continued. "Those kids who'd do anything for you for cookies and McDonald's?"

"They had nothing to do with this. I'd rather you left them alone."

Charlie shook his head. "They might have more information. We'll take good care of them."

Guilt filled her. She'd inadvertently involved those three innocents in this mayhem. Who knew how much this would impact their short lives. "There's three of them. Doran, Jaden, and Tiger. They are sweet kids. Don't mess them up."

Charlie gazed at Leona. "How do they know you? Why did they show up at your house?"

Repeating what she told Smythe, she said, "We met them when T-Bone threatened us. We made friends with them. Today, they walked over to my house to thank us for the food we bought for them. If you ask me, I think the reason they came was for more of Betty's chocolate chip cookies. They're nice boys, especially considering the place they come from."

Charlie told Smythe, "Take the cat lady around to see if the boys are here. Ask them where they were tonight. See if they can shed more light on this."

Smythe left to find Betty, and Charlie left to talk to other law officers. Two men pushed a gurney down the sidewalk to the ambulance. Leona leaned forward and put her face in her hands. She couldn't bear to see the poor girl's body go by. Had her actions caused someone to kill this girl? She hated her doggedness and her disregard of the advice telling her to forget the necklace and ring. If only she could go back in time, she'd never have started this crazy search for either of them. Joe would be extremely disappointed with her. How would she ever live with the guilt of having a part in the death of a young person? She never wanted to see the necklace again. It was forever cursed and should be melted down or thrown in to Mount Doom or something...anything to remove it from existence.

Her chest grew tighter and tighter, cutting off her air. Her head spun a little and she swayed in the seat. A hand reached out to steady her. She looked up to see Clarence with his walker. Black spots appeared in her vision, and her head became light. Her ability to sit upright left her.

Clarence pushed his walker toward her. "Put your head on my seat. You seem as pale as vanilla ice cream."

Resting with her head down helped her regain her sense of balance. She took slow, deep breaths as Clarence coached her to, and her senses were restored. Suddenly, she realized she had her face where Clarence often sat and sometimes passed gas. She shot up, but it made her dizzy again. This time she rested her elbows on the seat to hold her face away from the putrid vinyl.

Smythe returned and announced the boys confirmed her story. Betty wasn't with him but was probably feeding the boys cookies.

Charlie wrote a few notes in his notebook. "Okay, you can go, but don't leave town. You're still a person of interest."

Smythe heaved a sigh and ran his unsteady hand through his hair.

Did he always act this way at all crime scenes. Dealing with murder had to be hard on a person's psyche. Maybe he needed counseling and a vacation away from all his unsolved cases.

Not her problem, she decided, and rose from the car seat. Their performance tonight was probably the good cop/bad cop thing. She held onto the walker to make sure all her parts were working before moving it to where Clarence could reach it.

They shuffled through the night air. A crowd was still gathered behind the yellow tape, and lights lit up the yard. The flashing lights made it hard to see the ground clearly and Clarence nearly fell after tripping on the uneven sidewalk. The boys ran up and grabbed him around the waist and helped him along. Once they got Clarence into the minivan, the boys hugged the ladies.

Molly stood at the curb on the other side of the street. She called the boys over to her. She told them loudly enough for Leona to hear that they would be staying with her for the night.

Leona looked around for T-Bone. He was probably watching from the deep shadows. She'd watch her rearview mirror to make sure they weren't followed as they went home. She'd been stupid to go into his house. Another reason she wished she could go back in time.

Leona looked across the street where Molly stood, hands on her hips, and shaking her head. Three little heads peered around her before she turned her back and herded them down the sidewalk.

Leona's heart sank. The one person on this side of town whose respect she most desired was Molly's. From the looks of her reaction, she'd lost what little credibility she had with her. She turned the ignition and pulled away from the curb. One day, she'd come back and make amends with the kind woman.

CHAPTER 16

A slit of bright sunlight crept across Leona's bed and woke her when it reached her face. The room seemed brighter than normal. She glanced at the clock to discover she'd overslept by an hour. She didn't care. Getting out of bed wasn't a priority. Betty stirred in the kitchen, but no sound came from Clarence if he was there. Then she remembered. It was Sunday morning, the only day he didn't come over for breakfast.

Sunday mornings used to be a joyful occasion. She and Joe would lie in bed and talk about the week ahead. Then they would go to church and hear a wonderful sermon. After services, they'd join their church friends for lunch at the best buffet in town.

Leona smiled as the memories tickled her heart. She looked over at the empty pillow next to her. No ring. And it would never be there again. It was now a lump of gold. Just like that lump that was forming in her throat. A tear ran down her cheek and into her ear. It tickled. When another tear followed, she used the edge of the sheet to wipe it away.

The grief of losing Joe and now his ring made her heart hurt, but seeing her mother's favorite necklace around the neck of the dead girl was more than she could bear. She'd been wrong to pursue it so relentlessly. It may be her fault the girl was dead. All over a necklace and a ring. More tears followed, and soon the sheet edge was wet.

The sound of a platter shattering shook her out of her crying jag. Betty let out a cry of alarm, and Leona jumped out of bed, pausing long enough to put on her slippers. Running into the kitchen in her nightgown, she saw Betty in her robe crying at the table. Prissy circled in her lap for attention or comfort. Relieved that she hadn't found her sister on the floor with a heart attack, Leona sat beside her and hugged her shoulders.

"It's been a hard week, hasn't it," Leona said. She looked at the scattered pieces of a china plate Betty liked to use to serve cookies to friends.

Betty nodded. "Let's rest today after church. There's nothing pressing to be done."

"Good idea. Let's have a 'normal' Sunday. We'll go to services, and after lunch, we'll read the paper, maybe tend to the flowerbed, and watch TV. We haven't had much time to enjoy it. Let's break it in."

"I need to make more cookies. We've used a lot lately, and it helps me relax."

Leona agreed. "And maybe you'll find out where your kitty went." She smiled at her sister.

Betty laughed. "Ah, yes, my kitty. Things were getting much too serious, and I needed to lighten the mood. Faking dementia is the best way I know how to get everyone to step back and take a breath. And it worked." Betty's giggle was infectious, and Leona joined in.

"Yes, it did," Leona said wiping away the remnants of the morning's tears. "Smythe seemed too intense. I was afraid he was going to punch me or something."

Betty left Prissy on her chair, got the broom, and started sweeping the dish shards across the floor. "It's the advantage of being old. You can pretend to be senile and get out of a lot of trouble. If people think you're trying to get water out of a dry well, they usually give you anything to make you go away. It's like they're afraid your crazy will rub off on them." She bent over to sweep the pieces into the dustpan. "You can pretty much get your way if you know how to work it." Betty dumped the morning's disaster into the trash can.

"So, it's an act?"

"Most of the time."

"Keep doing it then."

Betty winked at her. "I will." She put the broom away.

Leona got up to get herself some coffee. "I'll have to remember that trick."

"Just don't act that way in front of your children, or they'll throw you into the Alzheimer's ward at a nursing home."

"Good point."

After church services, Leona, Betty, and Clarence accompanied their friends to a buffet restaurant for lunch. The waiters called them by name and visited with them when they came through the lines. Betty showed them her cane and exaggerated limp, so one carried her tray to their usual table in the back. The old friends brought their food and listened to the previous night's events as told by Clarence. Their shocked gasps and murmurs of concern filled their corner of the restaurant.

"Don't you feel guilty?" Carly asked her with raised eyebrows. "You got that poor girl killed. If it were me, I'd feel awful!" She stuffed a fork full of mashed potatoes into her mouth.

Irene slammed down her fork. "Carly! What a terrible thing to say! Of course, Leona feels terrible, but the murder was not her fault. Was it, Leona?"

Leona stared at the two women. She felt guilty about the girl dying but not as much as last night. Someone else had strangled her with her mother's necklace, not her. Plus, look where she lived and who her boyfriend was. A hardened criminal. According to the news reports, gang members occasionally killed each other over slight infractions. That must have been what happened to the poor girl.

"Well? Can you answer the question?" Carly looked at her over the top of her glasses. Her fork had a bite of salad on it, and she waved it in the air as if summoning an answer.

Leona didn't like being grilled by judgmental Carly, but she wouldn't be satisfied until she got the answers to her questions. "I feel bad, but it wasn't my fault. I wanted to talk to her about buying the necklace. I had the money in my pocket. If she'd stuck around at the flea market, I'd bought it from her there and she might still be alive." The scene from the house flashed through her mind. The line across her neck. The girl's empty stare. Her mother's necklace on top of a lifeless body.

Leona set her fork down, too queasy to continue eating. "I'm sorry for her, but she didn't keep good company. She was a pretty girl and could have done far better than T-Bone."

No one at the table spoke until Irene broke the silence. "I'm sorry for her too. I wish we could have done something to help."

Nick gave his empty plate to a waiter who came up to the table. "You should get a lawyer right away," he said, with the others nodding in agreement. "Talk to Ernie."

Betty laughed. "You'll never believe this about Ernie! He..."

"Shush!" Clarence said, "Don't gossip. We said we wouldn't say anything. Remember?"

"Oh right," Betty said, readjusting how she was sitting. "I'll just relate the facts. That's not gossip."

The ladies stretched across the table with eyes wide and eager ears. Betty whispered the plight of poor Ernie's wife. The women gasped at the anguish of Nancy, and the men snickered at Ernie's new life in Mexico. All agreed that it was a shame and sat back in their seats to let the buffet quantities settle before leaving.

George softly burped, then asked, "You still need a lawyer. Anyone know of another one that might be good?"

Clarence spoke up for the first time, "We talked with Triston Wilcox who bought Ernie's practice. He seems nice, but he's fresh out of law school. I'm not sure he has any experience with this sort of thing. He keeps saying he specializes in corporate law."

Irene spoke up. "You could use our lawyer. She's pretty good. She set up our trust and seems very knowledgeable about the laws."

Leona shook her head. "I don't need a trust. I need a criminal defense lawyer. Anyone ever worked with one of those?"

Everyone shook their heads. "None of us has ever done anything to need a defense lawyer," Carly said as she took a dainty taste of chocolate cake. The group watched as she chewed a little, swallowed, and then said, "Our friends usually don't have trouble with the law."

Nick jabbed his wife in the side with his elbow. "Leona is having trouble because she's innocent. She needs one to defend herself against wrongful charges."

Leona wanted to throw her cheesecake at Carly. She hadn't done anything to deserve a defense lawyer. Circumstances had thrown her into this unexplored territory. She needed a lawyer to help her find a way out of this mess. The words were on the tip of her tongue ready to escape when Betty broke the tension.

"Perry Mason!" Betty shouted. "That's who you need. He'd get the murderer to confess in court. What I wouldn't give to see that!"

"Still looking for that kitty?" Clarence winked at Betty.

Leona laughed while the rest of the group looked at each other and shook their heads. Left out of the joke, George and Irene began to gather their things to leave.

A surprise awaited the trio when they got home. On the front porch sat Jaden, Doran, and Tiger. They waved as they saw the minivan pull into the driveway. Betty was the first one out as she hurried to gather the boys into a hug. Leona fetched the walker for Clarence before hugging the boys and inviting them in.

"Have any cookies?" Tiger asked with his hands entwined like a beggar. "We're hungry."

"What happened to all that food we brought over the day before yesterday?" Clarence wheeled his way up the ramp.

Jaden piped up. "We're stretching it out, so it'll last longer. We wanted to try out our new shoes." He held out his foot so they could see them.

Leona went to the front door and unlocked it. "How did they work?"

"Good! We ran FAST in them!" Tiger ran to the end of the porch and ran back again. "Did you see how fast I went?"

"You were a blur!" Leona waved the boys inside.

"Wow! Your house is so big!" Doran looked all around her living room. His eyes were wide with amazement as he viewed the neat and tidy household. He ran his hands along the sofa cushions and lightly touched the lampshade beside it.

"Thanks, but it's just a regular house." Leona immediately regretted her words. New furniture. Freshly painted walls and new carpet. In their eyes, it must be a mansion.

The three boys were fascinated with everything. Doran seemed especially intrigued by the bookcase in the corner. He ran his hands over the spines of the books. "You got your own liberry."

Betty called them into the kitchen. "I might find a few nutritious things to heat up in the microwave." She told the boys to sit at the table while she pulled containers out of the refrigerator. "I'm out of cookies, but I could bake some while you eat lunch." The boys heartily agreed.

Leona sat at the table with them while Betty bustled around preparing lunch for the boys. "What brings you here? Does your mother know where you are?"

Doran ran his arm along the tabletop, feeling the surface. "She don't care where we are right now. She's fixing to do yard work again. We decided to come see you by ourselves."

"We like it over here." Tiger picked up the glass of milk Leona set in front of him. "It's so nice and clean and big." Doran frowned at his cousin and shushed him.

Leona covered her mouth with her hand lest something degrading about their mother come out in front of them. Their mother didn't deserve such good boys, and it would be by the grace of God if they stayed on the right path. Their fate may be up to her and Betty and Clarence, and especially Molly. Between the four of them, they could guide them to a better future.

Leona smiled at the boys. "We're glad you came to see us, but it's such a long way to come. It must be five or six miles. Did you really run all that way?"

Jaden put down his half-empty glass of milk. "We didn't run. We jogged."

Clarence sat in the fourth chair at the table and cleared his throat. "You boys could be in the Olympics marathon someday if you keep that up." He chuckled while the boys looked at him with their milk mustaches.

"What's Lympicks?" Tiger asked.

Clarence told them about the games as Betty finished heating lunch and Leona poured the last of the milk for the boys.

Betty put three plates of steaming leftovers in front of the boys who picked up their forks and dove in. "Wait! We haven't said grace yet. Clarence, will you please do the honors?" They all bowed their heads, and he gave thanks and a short blessing on the food. When they looked up, the boys looked confused.

"Can we eat now?" asked Doran with a mouthful of food.

Leona laughed and said yes. The boys dove in. "Don't you say grace before eating?" She put the empty leftover containers in the sink and ran water in them.

Jaden swallowed, then spoke. "No ma'am, but we're always thankful when we have something to eat." Their gratitude for the meal was evident by their smacking and MMMs of satisfaction.

Betty stirred up cookie dough while the boys ate, and the aroma of fresh baked cookies soon filled the kitchen. After they cleaned their plates, she invited them to help her put the balls of dough on the cookie sheet.

Leona picked up their empty plates to put them in the dishwasher. Seeing her open the door of the machine, Doran and Tiger ran over to watch. They wanted to help, so Leona let them put their own plates and silverware in and close the door. Their smiles and excited comments made the chore a pleasant one.

She sat down at the table as they ate the fresh-baked cookies. Leona leaned over close to Doran and broached the subject that had been weighing on her mind. "Tell me the real reason you boys came today. Is there something that we can help you with?"

Doran leaned forward, appearing to grow older as he did. "There's sumpin' we think you ought to know. That man last night. That man in the coat that was with Betty when she was talking to us. Is he really a policeman?"

Betty set another plate of warm cookies on the table. "You mean Detective Smythe? Tall, dark hair, gray suit coat?"

Doran bit into his third cookie. "Yeah." He took his time chewing, but finally continued. "We was afraid you wouldn't take us to McDonalds if we said anything when we was at the police station. We've seen him at that house."

Clarence and the ladies looked at each other, stunned. "He was probably there while he was investigating the crime on our house," Betty said. "Leona told him about her suspicions of him being the one who robbed our house "That's why he was there."

Doran thought a minute. "Maybe."

They waited for the rest of the story, but Doran was too engrossed in relishing his cookie to continue.

Clarence tapped his fingers on the table to get his attention. "How do you know this?"

Doran kept chewing and started to take another bite but thought better of it. "My uncle, Tiger's dad, he hangs around them sometimes, and I hear him talking. They try to get that man to help them, but he don't want to."

"Does your uncle help T-Bone rob houses?" Clarence asked.

"Sometimes."

"Does the policeman?"

Doran tilted his head. "Tiger's dad said he was mad at T-Bone and his gang for messing up something. They was talking about money and stuff."

Leona felt her body go limp as the boys' chatter muted for a moment. That would explain why Smythe seemed so nervous the other night. "Doran, I wish you had told us this at the police station."

His mouth full, he shrugged as he chewed. "I—" he swallowed a little, "I don't talk about what I hear. I keep my mouth shut so I don't get a beating. But I think you're in trouble, and I want to help you. I don't care if they give me a beatin' for telling you."

Leona stood up so fast, she knocked her chair over. The explosion of emotions inside overwhelmed her. Knowing Doran would sacrifice himself for her made her brain stop functioning. The thought of Smythe being involved with T-Bone fired it up again.

The boys stopped chewing and looked at her with puzzled eyes.

"Oops! I didn't mean to do that." She pushed the plate of cookies closer to them, then signaled Betty and Clarence to change the topic of discussion. She smiled at the boys and picked her chair up.

The boys were easily distracted by the treats. Leona had lots to say to Betty and Clarence, but that conversation would happen after the boys were back home. Back home on the same street as T-Bone. Did she dare take them back?

Smythe likely knew these boys and where they lived. He knew they were hanging around Leona, but he hadn't done anything to them. Yet. He could hurt them by putting them into separate foster homes far away where they couldn't harm him. She was helpless without a legal right to stop him.

That left only her, Betty, Clarence, and Molly to help them. They had to make a plan before something happened, whether they had the law on their side or not.

CHAPTER 17

Leona tried to keep a cheerful look on her face and in her voice as they took the boys home late that afternoon. She stopped by Molly's house, but no one was home, and the place was locked up tight. She couldn't leave the boys sitting on the front steps. Trouble lived in the neighborhood. Yellow crime tape around T-Bone's house still fluttered in the evening breeze.

At a loss to know what else to do, she drove two blocks over to their mom's house. Her conscience was screaming at her that this was a bad idea, but no other option presented itself. It was only for one night, she told herself. Tomorrow she would go see Tristan and start the process to get the boys out of here. He could tell her how to be their foster mother.

Once the boys were out of the minivan and in their hovel, Leona's rage bubbled freely and boiled over onto Betty and Clarence. "Do you think Smythe is dragging out the investigation because he's involved with it? I wonder if he knows who killed that girl and why? Is that why he wanted to blame me for it?"

Clarence cleared his throat. "Red Creek has a fine police department. I have a hard time believing one of them would be colluding with criminals. He's there investigating the crime wave he told us about."

Betty played with the handle on her purse. "Forget Smythe. Our boys may be in trouble because the gang knows they're friends with us."

Leona gripped the wheel with a steely hand as she turned the corner to head back to her side of town. Betty's thinking mirrored hers. Last night, Charlie Walters sent Smythe to talk to the boys. If Doran hadn't told what he'd heard, and he likely didn't, they might be okay. Charlie didn't know the predicament he'd put the boys in. Or was he part of that network, too? Was Rapid City also having a rash of burglaries?

The situation was grim. "I'm not sure what we can do to help them other than kidnapping. If Smythe found out what they told us, he'd get rid of them just like he did that girl."

"Leona!" Clarence said loudly, then lowered his voice. "That's preposterous! You may not like him, but he's not capable of murder."

"I don't know, but it makes sense. He killed her because she was wearing something I identified, and he was afraid I would connect him to T-Bone. His gang of thieves would unravel, and he would be implicated in their crimes. He would probably get sent to prison for that. No wonder he's so desperate to keep us out of the way."

"I think you're letting your imagination run amok." Betty let go of her purse handle and wrung her hands instead. "Smythe is a good guy doing his job. We should focus on the boys instead." She wiped her upper lip.

A yellow light appeared, and Leona stepped on the brakes. "They know too much for their own good. Maybe we should go back and get them. Their mother wouldn't miss them all that much."

"No!" Clarence said. "Smythe would call it kidnapping and have you in jail so fast you wouldn't know what happened. We must find another way."

He was right again, as much as Leona didn't want him to be. "Maybe their mother would agree to let us take them. We could talk to their mother when she's sober and tell her...."

A hush came over them and popped that balloon of hope.

Betty patted her chest, like she was trying to calm her heart. "That won't work. Finding her in her right mind would take too long."

Leona let out a loud sigh of frustration. She shook her head, trying to clear the whirlwind of thoughts swirling around in chaos. "I need to talk to a lawyer or go to the mayor or Child Protection Services. We can't call the police. There's got to be another solution."

Leona was at Tristan's office early Monday morning, waiting for him or Amber to show up. She went to a nearby coffee shop and got a coffee large enough to last until they arrived. An empty cup and an hour later, Amber drove up in her old rusty sedan that had

181

seen its better days more than two decades ago. She opened the office door and went in, followed closely by Leona.

Amber frowned when Leona told her to turn her computer on to find out what Tristan's schedule was for the day. Was he coming in or was he in court? With the speed of a turtle and eyes rolling like marbles, she complied with the request to find out that he was coming in later.

"That's no help." Leona sat in one of the chairs outside his office door. "I'll wait." She adjusted her new pantsuit jacket. Her purse always had a book in it for occasions such as this, but it held no interest to her. She needed to see Tristan now.

He came in about 30 minutes later looking like he'd just gotten out of bed. He carried his jacket and tie in one hand and a coffee cup in the other. His shoes appeared to be untied.

Oh brother! This man is a lawyer? Maybe she should check his credentials and make sure he'd passed the bar. She almost got up to leave, but decided to stay because she didn't know who else to approach about her precarious situation.

She sat in the chair in front of Tristan's desk while he sorted the coffee cup from his jacket and tie before plopping into his chair. He took a sack from his coat pocket, pulled out a pastry, and put it on the desk in front of him. Taking a sip of coffee, he asked, "What can I do for you, Leona?" He took a big bite out of the pastry before sitting back in his chair, rocking in rhythm with his chewing.

"The police are investigating me for the murder of the girl they found in the house of the burglary gang."

Tristan stopped rocking and chewing for a moment. He leaned forward while he finished chewing. "What?"

"They think I killed that girl."

He sat back and wiped his hands with a napkin. "Tell me what happened." He pushed the pastry aside, suddenly intent on listening to her story. When she finished, he said, "Did you kill her?"

"No! What an insane question!"

Tristan smiled. "I didn't think you did. You're not the sort. Do they have any evidence that you did it?"

"I don't think so. I first saw her when we met T-Bone, and then in that awful place, when Molly and I found her body. That's the extent of my contact with her."

He moved one shoulder. "Then they haven't charged you."

"Not yet. I'm worried Smythe may try to frame me for it. Saturday night, he acted like a madman and manufactured suspicions about me. They told me not to leave town." Leona leaned forward. "I have it on good authority that Smythe hung around T-Bone before that night. Maybe even conspired with that gang. Now I'm wondering if he murdered that girl."

"Who told you that?"

"I'd rather keep them out of this. They're just boys and have enough problems without adding killers to the mix."

"Boys? The same ones you talked to me about reporting to Child Protective Services?"

Leona sat back, uncomfortable with the turn in conversation. "Well, yes, but Doran is a reliable source. He may not be old on the outside, but he's an old soul. He observes and understands things beyond his years."

"How old is his outside?"

"Maybe eight or nine."

Tristan sat back, tapping his fingers together. "Is that all you got?"

"What more do you need? The kid says he's seen Smythe at that house and that he may be a part of the burglary ring. His uncle is part of the gang, and he's been talking where Doran could hear."

Tristan waved off her comment and took another bite of pastry. Leona could see his mind churning as he chewed. "So, what are you saying is you think Smythe killed the girl because he's the leader of the burglary ring?"

"I don't know about leader of the gang, but I think he's a crooked cop. He should be the one being investigated. Maybe the whole Red Creek police department is in on it."

Tristan's head jerked back. "This is a serious charge. Have you told anyone about your suspicions?"

"No one except Betty and Clarence." She thought a moment. "Oh, and Irene and George. And maybe Nick and Carly." She looked down at her hands and folded them differently. Her mouth was getting her in trouble...again. "I can't remember for sure. But I haven't said anything to Smythe about it."

"He's probably already heard it." Tristan took another bite of the pastry. He chewed a little. "Tell me more about this kid who told you about him."

"He's a boy that we met one day while looking for Joe's ring. He, his brother, and his cousin are sweet boys, and we felt sorry for them. We took food to their house and bought them clothes and shoes. They love Betty's cookies, so they sometimes walk over to our house to visit."

"And their parents are where?"

"Their mother is an alcoholic and a druggie. I'm not sure what else she is. Doran and Jaden haven't mentioned their fathers. I told you about Tiger's dad, but he's said nothing about his mother. When Doran told me he'd seen Smythe with that gang, I believed him."

"And his being there as part of his investigation didn't seem logical to you?"

"Maybe. But according to the boys, he was there before our burglary."

"Doesn't prove a thing. He's probably investigating other burglaries. Maybe he suspects the gang that lives there is committing the crimes. It makes sense."

"That's what Clarence and Betty say. But I get the feeling that he's not the good policeman like people think he is."

Tristan shook his head. He ate the last of his pastry and wiped his hands off as he chewed.

The effort to hold back a snarky remark took a lot of her strength. She looked away and squirmed in her chair while he finished his breakfast. His rocking and chewing made it hard for her to keep her tongue in check. Someone should teach him office and client manners.

Making a last big swallow, Tristan threw away the napkin. "You can't file a complaint based on feelings. We need concrete evidence or testimony."

"You're telling me to forget about it?"

"Unless you have something more than just feelings and a young boy's word, I recommend it. Chalk it up to personality conflicts and leave it alone. The truth will come out in the investigations."

"Not when a crook is doing the investigation."

"Then bring me hard credible evidence."

Leona looked at her hands as her shoulders slumped. Now what? If Tristan didn't believe her, likely no one else would either. She didn't trust Smythe, but no one believed her gut feelings were right. She dared not get Doran any closer to danger than he already was.

Tristan wiped the pastry crumbs from his shirt onto the floor. "As far as charging you with murder, it doesn't sound like they have evidence to do it. You should be cleared soon. If not, call me."

"Fine."

"And do this. Write everything down: dates, times, people, places. Document your actions and suspicions. I'll look at what you have and determine if you have enough evidence to file a complaint of police misconduct."

Leona wiped her slacks off, mindlessly emulating Tristan. "But he'll know who reported him."

Tristan agreed. "That's part of the process. He has the right to defend himself against his accusers."

"I'm not comfortable with that." Leona shifted in her seat as if pushing away from an unpleasant situation. "Maybe I shouldn't say anything."

Tristan leaned across the desk and looked intently at Leona. "It's your civic duty to report corruption. If something's going on that's illegal, we need to put a stop to it. But..." Tristan wagged his finger at her, "...if he's innocent, you're ruining a good man's reputation and livelihood. Falsely accusing a policeman is no small thing. You must be absolutely certain of what you're doing."

Leona sighed as she closed her eyes and rubbed her forehead. Was it worth the risk? What if she was wrong? Smythe didn't seem like the kind of man who would forgive and walk away. If it weren't for the boys, she'd drop it all. If Smythe made any move to hurt them, she'd—

"What if the boys came to live with me? My house is more secure than theirs. The police would arrive sooner if there was trouble. Could I be their foster mother?"

"Takes a while to become one. You have to submit an application, take classes, have your home inspected." He took another sip of coffee. "It takes time. Months, I've been told. Until then, you can report their living conditions to Child Protective Services who will put them into a certified foster home. Maybe later, after you're approved, they can come live with you."

"No! I won't have them split up or put into places where people wouldn't understand them like I do. They're good kids. I don't want a bad foster experience to mess them up."

Tristan held his hands wide. "I'm out of ideas."

Also, out of ideas and options, Leona had to relent to reality. The boys would have to fend for themselves, but they were used to it. Smythe might leave the boys alone as long as he didn't know what they had told her. He wouldn't risk being seen around T-Bone's house again. She rubbed her temples as the stress of the decision weighed heavy on her.

Tristan rattled some papers, signaling he was a busy man. "You don't have to decide this minute. Think about it for a day or two. And I feel I must remind you again, I'm not a criminal case lawyer. I specialize in—"

"I know. I know. Corporate law." Leona straightened her jacket. "I'll write things down so I can see what I have and come back later to talk about it."

Tristan held his hand up to stop her from leaving. "Just so you know, I'm going to have to start charging you for my time. I can't keep up this pro bono stuff unless I'm on a retainer with you. I hope you understand."

With dollar signs floating in her mind, Leona agreed and left.

CHAPTER 18

Leona stopped by the car wash on her way home. She sat back in her seat as the machines pulled her car through the water and soap. She wished they could wash away all her worries as easily as the power wash took away the dirt. She felt unclean and dirty after possibly having some role in the murder of a young woman. The stain would never leave her no matter the amount of scrubbing.

As she vacuumed the car out, several items under Clarence's seat clanked their way up the hose. She stopped the suction and felt under there, but her hand found nothing. She hoped it wasn't the hearing aid Clarence lost several months ago. Maybe it was rocks from his shoes or loose change he'd dropped when he paid for drinks at Sonic. Resuming her vacuuming, she didn't give it another thought.

The clean minivan lifted her spirits as she drove to the grocery store to pick up a few things. When she came out, she nearly dropped her bags when she saw Smythe leaning up against her car talking on his phone while other policemen stood by their cars blocking hers in.

Were they here to arrest her for murdering that girl? Here? Now? Red Creek was a small town where everyone knew who she was and now would think she was a felon. Her reputation would be ruined not only by gossips, but by the chief one of all, Carly. She'd gloat about how she was too smart to be taken in by a murderer. She'd known it all along. Leona's misfortune would be another feather in Carly's talebearer hat.

Torn between going back into the store to wait until he left or confronting him now, she gave in to the latter. She walked up to the minivan. "Why are you here?" Inside she was quaking, but he'd never see it if she worked it right.

He quickly hung up his phone. "We need to search your vehicle. Do you mind?"

"Yes, I do," she said. "What are you looking for? Got a warrant?"

He heaved an impatient sigh. "Yes." He pulled a folded paper from his jacket pocket and handed it to her. "I was hoping you'd cooperate. I'm looking for clues to a murder."

"In my minivan? I didn't kill that girl."

He raised one eyebrow. "Then you won't mind if I look."

Leona almost threw down her sack of groceries in anger, but she remembered the eggs and jar of pickled okra that were too expensive to break. She set the bags down gently on the trunk of the patrol car and nodded slightly as she unlocked the doors with the fob. She wasn't comfortable with their searching, but maybe they'd see that there was nothing in there to bring suspicion on her. Good thing she'd just cleaned it. They wouldn't find those French fries under her seat or the five-dollar bill she found under Betty's. Finders keepers.

Smythe looked in the front of the minivan first while the two policemen raised the back hatch to look in that compartment. One lifted the backseats out of the floor while the other let a drug-sniffing dog out of the police car. The dog jumped into the back of the minivan and sniffed around. He came out and went in the side door, sniffing all around. Leona held her hands up to protest but put them back down when she realized she could vacuum out the dog hair later. Might be worth paying for another car wash to get rid of Smythe's prints all over her minivan.

She watched Smythe search the front seat and glove box. Oddly, he didn't seem to look all that hard there. He looked in the backseat where Clarence usually sat. He ran his hand up under the seat. He seemed confused and searched there more vigorously. He stood outside the car with his hands on his hips, then repeated his efforts around Clarence's seat. She heard a low growl in his throat.

He walked to the back to talk with the other policemen in low tones. The three of them walked the dog back to the car where they continued to talk. After a short conference, the men went to their cars while another set her groceries in the back of her van before leaving.

Smythe came back toward Leona. "Okay, you're free to go," he said with clinched teeth. He slammed the minivan rear hatch with a vengeance of a frustrated man.

Leona winced as the door slammed shut. Her fists were clenched as she fought to control her anger. "Hey! Don't damage my van!"

Smythe didn't acknowledge her when he opened the door to his car.

Did he think he could do this and just walk away? She ran over to him before he could get in. "Just what did you think you'd find?"

He pressed his lips together and looked away. "We had a tip that there were drugs in your car."

His statement shocked her into silence for a split second before her rage came pouring out. "That's ridiculous! Not only that, but it's utterly ridiculous! Why don't you go search your friend T-Bone's car? Bang his car door off its hinges! Have you questioned him? He's probably the one who killed that girl."

His dark glasses hid his eyes, but his voice couldn't hide the strain in his tone. "We obviously were misinformed. I apologize for the mix-up. Just so you know, the investigation for the girl's murder is being handled by the Rapid City Police Department, not ours."

She didn't expect that. The yeast taken out of her dough, her temper couldn't rise up and make more accusations. She accepted his apology and retired to her minivan. She stared at Smythe's taillights as they lit up at the stop sign before turning the corner.

The scene kept replaying in her mind as she drove home. Smythe was frantic at one point and totally calm, almost kind at another. What was going on with him? Was she mistaken in suspecting him?

Her wall phone rang as she set the last bag of groceries on the kitchen counter. She yelled for Betty to answer it, but when she heard no response, she got it herself.

"Hello. I'm not interested in contributing to your cause or buying anything."

Silence followed. Leona was about to hang up when she heard a weak voice. "Leona?"

"Who is this?"

"This is Molly."

"Sorry about the awkward way I answered. So nice of you to call." Leona sat down at the table with the long cord stretched across the end of the counter. Prissy rubbed against her leg. What was up with the silly cat?

"Leona, are Doran, Jaden, or Tiger at your house?"

"Why no. I haven't seen them today. Why do you ask?"

"Their mom is over here wondering where they're at. They ate here last night, but I thought they went home afterwards, but you know that don't mean much. Those boys love to wander."

"They were here yesterday, but we took them home around four. It's not like them to be wandering around close to mealtime." It was nearly noon. Leona's heart started beating faster. The distance between the two houses was miles but they could have covered it by now. They could be anywhere in between. "Do you have any idea what route they'd take if they were coming over here?"

Molly let out a long sigh. "I don't know. They probably take shortcuts so they could be anywhere."

Thoughts eddied in Leona's mind. So many alleys, stores, parking lots, schools, churches, and houses were between the two homes. It would take hours to search them all. More importantly, were they okay? Those young boys should never be out on the streets like that.

"Molly, have you looked all over the neighborhood there?"

"Me and Kendra and my neighbor Hannah looked but didn't find 'em. Since they wandered over to your house a couple times, we were hoping they wandered over yonder again."

"Why don't you look around there more thoroughly, and I'll drive between here and there to look for them. Between the two of us, surely we'll find them."

"I'll call you if they turn up."

"Thanks, Molly, I'll bring them home if I find them."

Leona didn't take the time to look for Betty and Clarence. Leaving a quick note telling them where she'd gone, she left in her minivan and zigzagged through alleys, streets, parking lots, parks, and behind businesses to look for the boys. When she thought of different routes, she explored those as well.

At a red light, she closed her eyes and rubbed her temples like she always did when anxiety took over. She didn't want to quit looking for the boys, but she didn't know where else to look.

A honk from the car behind let her know that the light was green. She had no alternative but to face the boys' mother. She would be furious again and the language out of her mouth would sting Leona's ears. It was no less than she deserved. She should have made it clear to the boys not to come over without asking permission or telling someone where they'd gone. She'd rewarded their wandering behavior with new clothes, shoes, and food. Her charitable heart had encouraged the boys to continue their long walks through town.

She parked in front of Molly's house in time to see Kendra dashing out of the house toward the minivan. Leona tried to see if there was a smile or a frown on her face. She hit the side of the minivan as Leona turned the motor off and got out.

"We can't find 'em." Kendra was huffing and puffing. "Me, Grandma, and Zilo just got back from running all over, hollering at 'em to come home."

Molly came outside and waved at Leona to come in. Kendra put her arm around Leona and walked beside her to the steps.

All the children she'd met on the north side of town seemed to want to touch her and hug her. What kind of attraction did she have to them? Maybe it was nothing more than knowing that she might buy things for them. Or could it be something deeper, more basic? Love itself? She loved children which is why she taught elementary school for so many years. Since retiring, she missed being with children and their hugs. She gave Kendra a warm squeeze as she walked up the steps into the house.

Lila was being held back by the strong arm of Molly. Her brow was furrowed, and her mouth was covered by Molly's hand. Kendra took off like a scared rabbit.

Molly yelled at Lila, "This is MY house, and it's a Christian home. No profanity allowed in here. If you wanna say something, it better be clean, or I'll throw your good-for-nothing backside outta here. You understand?"

Leona backed down the steps in case she needed to escape. Molly seemed to be in control as she turned to look at Leona. "Did you find the boys?"

"I looked everywhere I could think of and nothing." She squeezed her eyes together to hold back the gathering tears. "I'm sorry. I should have never gotten this routine started, where they come over to my house whenever they take a mind to."

Lila pushed Molly's arm aside and broke free from the strength of the larger woman. "You're trying to take my boys away from me! I won't let you! They're mine!"

"Settle down, Lila!" Molly pushed the woman back a step. "Your boys have wandered all over town since the day they were born. If they wandered off today, it's nothing but your own doing. If you was sober and a real mother to them, they'd stay home like they oughta. Leona didn't have a thing in the world to do with it."

The bloodshot eyes of the angry woman conveyed her lack of emotional or physical control. "She buys them things to draw them away from me!" Lila looked at Leona with hatred and fire in her eyes. Her hand was clenched like a claw, threatening to tear into Leona's skin. The hand reached in her direction and waved in the air like a tiger's paw.

Molly pushed Lila back another step.

Leona took a step back and got ready to run as fast as her old legs would go. Lila would easily overtake her, but she'd try to find soft ground to fall on.

Leona fought her fear and tried to stay calm. "I'm not trying to pull them away from you. I didn't invite them to come over. They came of their own accord." Leona waved her hands in the air. "We can argue about this later. First, we need to concentrate on finding them."

Molly agreed just as Kendra came running up on the porch, nearly knocking Leona down. "Grandma! Miz Maria saw the police take the boys away. She said they was over in the park, and a police car stopped and talked to them. She said Doran fought against the policeman and Jaden and Tiger tried to run away, but another policeman caught them, and they took them all away."

Leona's heart froze. Smythe. He had the boys. She put her hand over her mouth to keep a cry of distress from escaping. Doran must have known they were in trouble if he told his brothers to run. She could hardly breathe. She began to wobble and collapsed on the porch steps.

"They got my boys!" Lila screamed into the neighborhood. "They won't never give 'em back neither." She let out a bawling howl.

Molly told Kendra to get a glass of water as she knelt beside Leona. Kendra dashed back with one.

As she took it, Leona hoped the glass was clean before drinking. Her head spun so much that she needed the water more than she cared about germs. She thanked the girl for bringing it to her and sipped it. The tepid water did little to calm her nerves.

Lila stood on the porch ready to take on Leona. "This is your fault!"

Leona wailed through the growing stream of tears. "I'm so sorry. I never meant to get them involved in my search for Joe's ring. I never intended any harm to anyone." She wiped her eyes. "Don't worry. I'll get my lawyer on it, and we'll have them out in very short order." She took another sip of water, then gave the glass back to Kendra.

She noticed Zilo standing in the doorway, staring at the adults with wide, scared eyes.

Lila stood with her fists clenched. "You got a lawyer?"

"Yes, and he'll get them out."

Molly sat beside Leona. "Lila, you go on home. Leona will make sure your boys get back. She cares for them as much as you and I do. Now go on."

Lila shuffled her feet as if they were arguing with each other over which one should take the first step. She pointed her shaking finger at Leona. "You get my boys out of jail and never come back. You hear me? Stay away from them!" Her jaw worked with profanities, but one look from Molly kept them unsaid. She slumped on the porch and pulled her knees up to her chest.

Leona's heart was about to jump out of her chest. Lila had frightened her so much that she felt faint. If it hadn't been for Molly's strong presence, she might have fainted from fear and anguish over the boys. She dropped her head in her hands.

"She's right. It's all my fault."

"You said you'd call your lawyer to get 'em out."

Tristan. She had to call Tristan. Her dizziness subsided with the call to action. She'd get Tristan right on it. Looking around for her purse, it was nowhere to be seen. Molly sent Kendra out to the minivan to see if it was there. Soon she came bouncing in with her purse over her shoulder. Hunting through the bag, she found her phone and dialed Tristan's number.

CHAPTER 19

Leona drove in the garage next to the Eldorado soon after her call to Tristan. The house was quiet except for Prissy who circled her feet as she tried to walk. Betty was still nowhere to be seen. Puzzled, she looked around for a note from her sister explaining where she'd gone. As she headed for the living room, the phone rang.

"Leona, this is Tristan," came the voice on the phone. "I called the police station and found out they picked up three boys who were wandering unsupervised in your neighborhood. They were taken into custody on suspicion of burglarizing homes. They were the ages you indicated so they're probably your boys they picked up."

Leona's voice got stuck. Not Doran, Jaden, and Tiger! Who on earth would think those sweet boys could do something like that, especially boys that young?

"Tristan, it's a lie! They weren't picked up in my neighborhood. I just got back from Molly's and a lady down the street from her saw the police pick them up in a park on the north side."

"Are you sure?"

"Absolutely sure! Something's not right. Go to the police station and find out what's going on. Those boys are NOT thieves! It's Smythe! He thinks they'll rat him out by pointing the finger at him for his associations with T-Bone. He's the one who murdered that girl! She gave him away by wearing my necklace."

"Calm down, Leona! You're talking crazy again. No one knows who killed that girl. Stop making accusations you can't back up before you get sued for slander."

"Either do what I say, or I'll do it myself! Go down there and check on those boys! Oh my! What they must be going through." Leona paced around the kitchen with the phone pressed to her ear and almost tripped over Prissy. Dumb cat. She was ready to toss it outside, but first things first. "We've got to help them. I'll go to the police station and confront Smythe—"

"No! That will make things worse for them." Tristan was silent for a moment. When he spoke, his voice was calming. "I'll check on them and call you back as soon as I know something. In the meantime, stay home."

"They need a lawyer so you're it. Don't let one of those cheap public ones do the job. You represent them, and I'll pay their fees."

"Leona, I keep telling you. I'm not a criminal—"

"You are now! Go and see about those boys!"

She called Molly to let her know the news. In the background, she could hear Lila cursing her, Molly, the police, and anyone else who came to mind.

Leona didn't care. The entire world could be angry with her. The important thing was knowing where the boys were. She had to have faith in Tristan to handle their troubles.

She ran across the street with Prissy on her heels looking for Clarence. To her surprise, Betty opened the door holding a large garbage sack. Clarence was in his chair with a lap full of magazines. "Oh, here you are! What are you doing?"

"I'm helping him clean his house," Betty looked surprised anyone would ask. "Hello, my Prissy." She bent down and snuggled the cat into her arms.

A multitude of stacked magazines and newspapers lay around the room. "Yes, I see. We don't have time for that now. Come on! The boys have been hauled to the police station because they think they're thieves. Tristan says they've been charged with burglarizing people's houses. I think Smythe is doing it to them to get to us. You know what else he did? He searched my minivan! Imagine my embarrassment at having my vehicle ransacked by that...that..."

"Scofflaw?" Clarence looked pleased with himself for being a nearby thesaurus.

Wondering where he'd learned that word, she used it in a sentence. "We have to save the boys from that scofflaw."

Betty put down her garbage sack and went to Leona. "Did you call Tristan? He might be able to help."

"He said he'd check into it and call me back. Told me to stay home."

"You should go back to the house and wait for his call. He'll know what to do and how to handle it. You can't go storming down there to demand answers and expect to get any." Betty looked at Clarence who nodded in agreement. "He might be calling the house right now."

"Stay here if you want." She turned to go. "I'm going to the rescue."

The plastic bag fell to the floor as the walker began to squeak its familiar tune.

"You three again?" The desk sergeant threw down the papers he was carrying. Leaning toward the plexiglass, he said, "I told you before! We're working on it. Now go home and leave me alone!"

Leona slammed her purse down. "Don't get curt with me, mister! We're here on another matter. You arrested three innocent boys, and I want them released into my custody. I'll be responsible for them. I'll pay their bail or whatever you need to let them go."

"I don't know who you're talking about. What boys?"

Betty stepped up beside Leona and opened her purse. She leaned her cane against the wall, pulled out a little bag full of cookies, and set them in front of the opening in the plexiglass between them. "Their names are Doran, Jaden, and Tiger. They're cute as buttons!" She wrinkled her nose at him.

The sergeant looked at the ladies and at the cookies. He rubbed his forehead, then pushed the cookies back toward Betty. "Are you bribing me for information about an arrest?"

Betty tittered. "This is no bribe. You look hungry, and these are going to waste in my purse. Wouldn't you like one or two or five?"

The sergeant balked, but the cookie temptation overtook him. He gently lifted one of the cookies out of the bag, barely holding it with his fingertips. He took a nibble from it and a look of deliciousness flashed across his face. He quickly masked his opinion and finished the cookie in record time.

"Could you be talking about those boys who were arrested by Detective Smythe? He said they robbed your house."

"No, they didn't!" the trio shouted in unison, drawing the attention of several other officers behind the counter.

Leaning forward, Leona lowered her volume to say, "I'm sure of it. Smythe wants them off the street because they can place him at the scene of the murder."

The sergeant reached for another cookie. "I don't know anything about a murder. He brought the boys in because he found evidence on them. They had a string of pearls that you reported missing. He caught them red-handed." He bit into the cookie with relish. "They're guilty all right."

Leona's hand went to her chest as she gasped. "My pearls? They had my pearls?"

"Can't be true." Betty shook her head.

The sergeant bit into another cookie. He told them to wait there while he went into the back.

The trio huddled together. "Smythe framed them," Leona said. "I'm sure of it. He's trying to take them out of the picture."

Clarence frowned and cleared his throat. "But if they really did have your pearls, Smythe had no choice but to arrest them. He couldn't ethically ignore the evidence."

Betty's brows furrowed. "What if T-Bone gave them the pearls, and they were on their way to return them to us? Maybe that's what happened."

Both scenarios could be right, and Leona knew it, but her opinion of Smythe couldn't be changed. "Maybe Smythe had them and slipped them to the boys when he arrested them. They're too innocent to understand what entrapment is. Tristan can use that to get them out. I should call him." She dug in her purse. "Where's that phone now that I need it!"

As she was rummaging, the sergeant returned with a manila envelope. He opened the end and slid the contents out on the countertop. A single strand of pearls rolled across. Betty let out a soft cry of surprise and picked them up.

"These are yours, Leona!"

"There you have it, folks." The sergeant crossed his arms. "Can't fight evidence. Smythe found these on the boys. They're guilty all right."

It couldn't be true. Maybe it was a bad dream. Leona pinched the roll around her waist. She felt it. It wasn't a dream, but none of it made sense. "No, they're not thieves! They were framed! Smythe planted the pearls on them!" Leona pounded the counter in frustration.

Betty pulled the bag of cookies toward her, but the sergeant reached out and grabbed another one before she put them away.

He scowled at Leona. "Look, lady, I've been as nice as I can be to you for as long as I can. This crazy idea of yours about our Detective Smythe has gone far enough. You're losing your mind and getting senile or something, but Smythe would never do something like that. He's one of the good guys!"

"I know otherwise. You're protecting your own, even to the detriment of innocent children." She picked up her purse.

"You're nuts, lady!" The desk sergeant stuffed the pearls back into the manila envelope. "That man has been through a lot. His wife died of cancer last year. Did you know that?"

Leona felt a stab in the heart. Anyone losing a spouse, even an enemy, had her sympathy. She missed Joe badly, and Smythe probably missed his wife as much as she missed her Joe. She felt a pang of guilt for being so nasty to him.

The desk sergeant went on. "Her chemo cancer treatment cost over $12,000 each time, not to mention the cost of surgeries. He sold everything he could to raise the money. He remortgaged their house. We all pitched in to help as much as we could, but she didn't make it. He's been left with all those bills. Don't you think he's had enough heartache without an overbearing, crabby complainer harassing him?"

Betty sniffed. Clarence cleared his throat but said nothing. While Leona's heart went out to Smythe, her focus was on her boys.

"No sob story is going to make me change my mind. Those boys had nothing to do with burglarizing our house. I want to see them! They'll tell me the truth. Where are they? I want to talk to them."

The desk sergeant sat down on his tall stool and bit into his cookie. "Are you their lawyer, parent, or guardian?"

"No. I'm the overbearing crab who they are supposed to have robbed. I deserve to see my thieves."

"It doesn't work that way. They're minors. Unless you're a parent or a guardian or their lawyer, you can't see them."

Leona wasn't sure what to do next. She could pound on the desk and demand to be taken to see them. She could ask for the police chief and complain about the poor quality of service. She could even start saying "here, kitty, kitty" in hopes he'd think she was crazy and let her have anything she wanted. She threw out the last option, scared they'd escort her to a rubber room instead.

Betty took her by the arm. "Tristan can go see them."

Clarence took her elbow. "Let's go talk to him. Maybe he can get in and see them."

Leona stood firm, yet knew she was defeated. The young lawyer who couldn't sit still for a minute and had no sense of customer protocol was her last hope.

Betty got a firmer grip. "Let's go, sis, before you make more trouble."

Unable to fight against it, she jerked her elbows away from them and stomped her foot while facing the desk sergeant. "You tell Smythe he better not hurt those boys. I'm as sorry as I can be about his wife, but my focus is on the wellbeing of those boys. I can cause him a lot of trouble, and I'll do it if he so much as touches a hair on their heads." Turning, she lifted her chin. "Come on, gang. Let's get out of this sorry place."

CHAPTER 20

"Don't tell me to calm down!" Leona paced in the living room of her home. Occasionally she would stop, sit down, and think. The frustration didn't let her sit long. She would let out a cry of aggravation and begin pacing again. Her jaw ached from clenching, and her foot had a dull ache from stomping.

Tristan sat on the edge of one of the new recliners, watching his client meltdown. Betty sat on the sofa with her crocheting project in her hands. Clarence sat next to her watching Leona wear a pace pattern on the new carpet.

Tristan stood up and tried to stop Leona's pacing. She shook him off and continued to pace while wringing her hands. He sighed and threw up his hands. "There's no evidence for what you're saying about Smythe. You could be wrong—"

"I'm not wrong!" Leona stopped and glared at the young lawyer.

Tristan held his hands up in surrender and sat back down on the edge of the recliner. "We've reached a dead end. We can't go forward without something to go on. The law needs more than your gut feeling. There's nothing else I can do."

Leona tsked him as she paced. "Perry Mason would have found a way. So would Matlock."

Tristan closed his eyes and pinched the bridge of his nose as he crinkled his face. "Those are fictional stories written by people and solved in an hour. If anyone suspects you don't know the difference between TV and real life, the boys will be the least of your worries."

Silence filled the room while Leona stopped to stare at the guest who sat where Joe's recliner once sat. Was he implying she was crazy? How dare he! She hadn't even called an imaginary kitty yet. She gave him a look she hoped made molten lava seem icy. It worked. Tristan squirmed uncomfortably under the intense heat.

Betty looked up from her project. "I bet you didn't figure on getting into this kind of mess when you bought Ernie's practice, did you, Tristan." She smiled at him and gave a soft chuckle.

One side of Tristan's mouth rose a little. "No, I thought I was buying a nice quiet practice where most of my clients would want help with their businesses or the city might want a lawyer on retainer. I'm not prepared for criminal law."

"Well, you better get prepared for it, buster!" Leona started pacing again. "Three boys are depending on you to set things straight."

"Leona, dear," Betty said, "why don't you get us some iced tea. It's hot in here, and I'm thirsty."

She stamped into the kitchen and opened the freezer door. The cool air chilled her face and temper. Alienating the only lawyer she trusted at this point in time would be detrimental to her goal of helping the boys. The heat of her ire dissipated. She filled four tall glasses with ice and tea and carried them back into the living room.

Handing a glass to Tristan, she said softly, "I'm sorry. The boys mean a lot to me. I'm depending on you to set things straight. Please."

A look of resignation came across Tristan's face which released itself through a heavy sigh. "I've got contacts that might be able to help me. A friend from college went into criminal law. Maybe he has advice for this situation."

"Good!" Betty clapped her hands together. "Everything's settled! By the way, Tristan, you should watch those lawyer shows and get some ideas on how to be a good lawyer. You can expand your skills, and Leona will quit wearing a hole in the new carpet. To celebrate, how about some cake all around?" She used the cane to help her up off the sofa before trotting off to the kitchen.

Tristan stood and said, "I need to be going. I have a lot of homework to do."

Betty came hurrying back and grabbed him. "Oh, but I make such good chocolate cake."

"Chocolate?" Tristan's eyes were wide like a child's when seeing his birthday cake.

"Betty," Leona said in a voice she used with her children, "Tristan said he has homework. We should let him get to it."

His eyes moved between Leona and Betty before his shoulders slumped slightly. "Yes, I do. I'll take a raincheck on that cake. I have phone calls to make and books to consult."

CHAPTER 21

Leona put the last of the supper dishes in the dishwasher and closed the door. While wiping off the counters, she reviewed her mental list of what needed to be done. First, she had to find a way to control her impulses while Tristan worked to free the boys, but then what? They couldn't—or shouldn't—go back home. Her stomach hurt to think about them living in that firetrap of a house with a mother who loved them, she hoped, but was incapable of taking care of them. Her heart couldn't fathom the thought they were nothing more to her than additional Welfare payments.

But where else could they go? Foster care? Being separated would be traumatic for them. Doran mothered his brother and cousin and seemed to have done a good job at it. Taking them away from him would be like taking kids from their parent—just like she was plotting to do.

Maybe she should leave well enough alone. They'd done okay with their circumstances. She could supply them with necessities like food and clothing. Molly's home was a place of refuge, and she could keep an eye on them and call when they needed help. They might do better with that than being taken into foster care.

213

Yet being exposed to the bad people in the neighborhood and their mother's vices wasn't good for them.

She scrubbed the same place on the countertop as her mind replayed a reel of the past weeks. Her misplaced determination had caused the whole mess. Everyone told her to step away, but like a scaly, overweight alligator, she'd clung and twisted and gotten so tied up in the whole mess, she couldn't let go. All she'd achieved was to upset the boys' lives and maybe even gotten that girl killed over her mother's necklace. The responsibility landed firmly on her shoulders.

Nausea swept over her, and she leaned over the sink. She gasped in great gulps of air that slowly began to make her head swim. Hyperventilating wasn't going to help. She needed to lie down.

She rinsed out her dishrag and spread it out to dry. The day's unread newspaper was on the table. She picked it up and headed to her new recliner in the living room to read it. She needed to relax and get her mind off her problems.

Walking into the living room, the sight on the sofa stopped her in her tracks. Her mouth fell open as she saw Clarence and Betty sitting close. Too close. Clarence's hand brushed Betty's knee. Betty giggled. Not her usual giggle, but a schoolgirl giggle. Clarence's arm went around her and pulled her closer.

Prissy sat on the end of the sofa away from her usual place in Betty's lap. The look she gave Leona reflected disgust. She hopped off the sofa and ran past Leona standing in the doorway.

Leona blinked, not wanting to believe what she was seeing. When she heard the word 'kissie-poo,' she spun around, followed Prissy down the hallway, and rushed toward her bedroom.

She flopped onto her bed and put the newspaper over her face. Was the world going mad? Innocent boys in jail. Bad cops. Incompetent lawyers. Now Betty and Clarence.

She didn't even want to think about the last one. Her stomach felt uneasy. Still under the paper, she did the only thing she could think of—she prayed. After enumerating her concerns and requests, she said a loud "Amen" and felt better.

Laying on Joe's side of the bed, she turned on the lamp, opened the newspaper, and tried to focus on the stories. The usual town headlines were there: city council bickering, desperately needed street repairs, crime in the streets. She turned to the comic section, hoping for a chuckle.

In an instant, her ears were overwhelmed by the deafening thunder of glass and other things exploding and breaking. She heard Betty let out a hoarse scream. Clarence yelled out something she couldn't understand. The noise seemed to go on forever, but died away when the sound of squealing tires reached her ears. After that, only the sound of dogs barking broke the eerie quiet.

Leona grasped her chest to keep her heart from pounding its way out as she rose from the bed. She yelled out Betty's name as she ran down the hallway toward the living room but heard no response. Running through the kitchen and into the living room, the sight nearly made her faint. Her picture window was gone. The shredded curtains moved like fringe in the breeze. Her new TV

215

screen was blown to bits, with only the shell of it on the wall. Glass was everywhere, large pieces, pointed shards, and slivers glittered across her carpet in the lights from the kitchen. The walls were full of holes. The air smelled of smoke and blood.

On the floor, Betty lay with her eyes closed. Blood ran down her face. Her sleeve was turning red. Clarence was slumped over on the sofa. His blood dripped onto the upholstery.

A cry of alarm escaped her throat without her bidding it. She ran to the back door to slip on her shoes. Rushing to Betty's side, she knelt and felt her neck. A soft beating pulsed under her hand, eliciting a short sigh of relief. She stroked Betty's hair softly and whispered that everything would be all right.

Someone pounded on the door, yelling to be let in. Leona recognized the voice of her neighbor and rushed to the door to open it. A middle-aged man in his pajamas, came in and gaped at the scene.

"Jason, call 911! Hurry! They're hurt!" Leona screamed out as she rushed back to Betty.

"I already have," Jason said as he rushed to her side. "I'll check Clarence. He looks bad!" As he moved to the sofa, the faint sound of a siren drifted in through the shattered window.

Another neighbor, then another came through the door. Leona shouted for someone to get towels from the kitchen. Another man helped Jason move Clarence so they could apply pressure to his wounds.

Leona couldn't force any more words through her tears. Leona lifted Betty's reddening sleeve. Blood oozed out of a hole in her skin, repulsing Leona, and she looked away for something to stop the bleeding. Her neighbor John knelt beside her and put a hand-embroidered towel over the hole. "Let me hold this firmly against her arm. That should help slow the bleeding," he told her.

Grateful for someone else to take charge, she did as she was instructed. The siren was getting closer, and the tension in Leona eased. Medical help was almost there. She swallowed the terror in her throat and managed to say, "How's Clarence?"

Jason's face was pale and damp with sweat. "I don't know. He's been hit several places, and his pulse is very faint."

A wail erupted from Leona. "Who could do this to us? We haven't done anything!" She sucked in her breath as she thought about Smythe. She shook her head. He might be a bad cop, but even she didn't believe he was capable of something like this. It must have been T-Bone and his thugs. They were the kind who'd shoot at innocent people to shut them up.

Red strobe lights flashed around the room, making her dizzy and lightheaded. At the same time, she was comforted. Help was here. Those who knew what to do could take over and make her sister and Clarence well again.

Betty's lips began to move. Leona bent over so she could hear what her sister was trying to say. At first, it was too faint, but then she heard the words. "Here, kitty, kitty."

217

Leona sat in a waiting room, staring at the floor, her mind down the hallway where Betty was being examined. Clarence had already been wheeled into surgery. She'd called his son Tom and Betty's daughter Diane, and both were on their way. The hardest call was to her daughter Jennifer who was also on the way. She made one more call to Irene who would spread the word to their friends. At this point, nothing was left to do but wait and pray.

Wait and pray. She'd waited and prayed in this same room while they worked on Joe two years ago. He'd collapsed at home clutching his chest. The EMTs came and rushed him to the hospital. All she could do then was wait and pray. When the doctor finally came to see her, his face told her the story. No words had to be expressed. Her Joe was gone.

Here she was again. The dread and fear inside her were overwhelming. She didn't want to see the doctor, afraid of what his face would hold. Afraid of losing her sister. Afraid of being alone.

To take her mind off her feelings, she focused on the smell of cleansers, the sounds of nurses and people going by, the loudspeakers asking for help in other departments, and other people waiting to hear news. The exercise only made her more uncomfortable.

Her jitters wouldn't let her sit long, so she paced back and forth until she was too tired to walk any more. She sat on the edge of a chair, afraid to look down. Her pants and blouse were stained by Betty's blood, and she couldn't stand the sight of them. She craved a shower and her soft warm bed and Joe's ring to comfort her.

Irene and George were the first to arrive, followed by Nick soon after. George wore a wrinkled tee shirt tucked into a pair of sweatpants. Judging from the sweater Irene had on and how she crossed her arms all the time, she hadn't bothered to put on a bra. Nick apologized for Carly's absence. He didn't want to wait for her to get fixed up before coming.

They offered her coffee, food, hugs, and words of encouragement. They didn't press her for details but listened as she told them about the noise, the blood, the fears. She only faintly heard their remarks because her own thoughts were so loud. The questions tumbled in her mind like clothes in a dryer, round and round, tumbling over and over. Why, why, why... Who would do this, who would do this, who would do this... It should have been me, it should have been me, it should have been me...

A firm hand on her shoulder brought her out of her turmoil. She looked up into the worried face of Tristan. "Who told you?"

"George called me. I wanted to let you know that I'm here for you."

"Thanks." Her eyes watered, blurring the scene. She put her hand over his and squeezed. "I should have listened to you."

Tristan sat beside her. "I've spoken to the police. They think T-Bone and his gang are responsible, but they can't find them. When they do, they'll be brought in and questioned. No charges have been made yet. Part of that will depend on Betty and Clarence."

"Depend on them? Do they have to formally press charges?"

"No. I mean the police don't know yet what kind of charges they'll file against whoever did this." He looked around at her circle of friends, as if willing the others to read his mind so he didn't have to say the words. "You know, assault with a deadly weapon or—or—maybe something more serious."

Irene let out a loud gasp. "Or murder!" she cried out before starting to weep. George quickly put his hand over her. "Try to get a hold of yourself!"

Irene quickly went to Leona and put her arms around her. "Now, Leona, don't worry, dear. I'm sure they'll both be fine, and we'll be laughing about this before you know it. Well—maybe not laughing but talking about it." She patted Leona and turned to glare at Tristan. "Don't you know what Leona has been through tonight? She's very delicate right now."

"You said it, not me."

Leona shushed them both and gently pushed Irene away from her. "I've already thought about that possibility. If Smythe investigates, it will go nowhere. Can we get someone else, an impartial investigator to look into it?"

Tristan cracked a slight smile. "You get your wish. Detective Charlie Walters from Rapid City does homicides and assaults."

Leona felt relieved. "First good news of the day."

A scrub-clad young man sauntered in the door. "Leona Walker?" He scanned the crowd that had gathered. Fingers pointed at Leona in the chair. "Are you Betty Drummond's sister? She's asking for you."

Leona stared back at him, looking for any hint of his next words. His face held no darkness, and his voice's tone held no bad news. Her heart felt a small glimmer of hope. "Is she going to be alright?"

The young man smiled. "Yes, she's fine. She has some bruises and a lot of cuts that should heal. A bullet went through her upper arm, but it missed the bone and did little damage. A few weeks rest and she'll be good as new. She's a very lucky lady."

A flood of tears threatened to break lose, but Leona blinked them away. She allowed herself to breathe again. Praise the Lord! Betty would live! Sounds of joy and prayers of thanks filled the room until someone asked, "How's Clarence?"

It came suddenly, like a thunderstorm. A dark cloud covered the young man's face, and Leona knew his next words would be terrible. She felt her chest tighten again, preventing her from taking another breath.

"I can't divulge his condition except to next of kin," he said. "But I will say this, he needs your prayers."

CHAPTER 22

"Leona?"

The sound came from nowhere yet was everywhere. It called her, but she didn't have the strength or will to answer it.

"Leona. Wake up."

As her unsettling dream faded, Leona stirred and wondered why her back and neck hurt so much. She reached to rub her neck and realized she was sitting in a chair. Flickering her eyes open, she looked into the face of Betty in the hospital bed next to her. She jumped out of the chair, but the dizziness made her drop back into the seat. She grabbed the arms of the chair to steady herself.

"Should I call the nurse?" Betty asked as she reached out toward Leona.

"No, I just stood up too fast." Leona stood again, slowly and carefully, hanging on to the sides of the bed. "I'm fine. How are you feeling? You have a little more color in your face."

"I feel weak and hurt all over, like I've been run over by the ice cream truck." Betty moved her arms until Leona took them gently and held them still.

"Don't do that! You don't want to pull this IV out of your hand." Leona smoothed the tubes to make sure they weren't pulling on the needle on the back of Betty's hand and that she was getting all the oxygen she was supposed to get. She clasped the hand without the IV and held onto the cold fingers, trying to warm them with hers.

Tears welled in Betty's eyes. "What happened? I can't remember. I just remember noise. Loud noises and getting pushed off the sofa. I don't understand."

A tear fell from Leona and landed on the bed beside Betty. "It's all my fault. Mine alone. I should have never started my crazy search for Joe's ring. Smythe was right. We got into things that we had no business being around. And now you and Clarence are hurt— "

The door swung open as a cheerful young nurse came in. "I see you're awake. Good! Let's take some vitals and see how you're feeling." She proceeded to punch the buttons on the monitor and gather information as the blood pressure cuff on Betty's arm swelled. "What is your pain level?"

Leona got a tissue and gave one to Betty. "Pretty sore," Betty said after wiping her eyes. "Maybe a five."

"Do you want a little pain medication?"

Betty shook her head. "No, it makes me crazier than I am. I just want aspirin so I can go home to recover in my own bed. My sister can take care of me."

The nurse smiled. "I think you'll be able to go home today, but the final word comes from the doctor. He'll be in later."

She finished her vitals gathering and asked before leaving, "Need anything?"

Betty nodded. "I need to know how my friend Clarence Brown is doing. Can you tell us?" A look of concern flashed across the nurse's face as she came back to the bedside.

"He's not on this floor so I don't know much about it. I'm sure he could use your prayers." She patted Betty's arm softly and gave Leona a weak smile. "Need anything else?"

Betty grabbed the nurse's arm before she could pull away. "Why can't you tell us? He was Leona's husband's best friend from childhood. He's all alone in town and needs us."

"I'm sorry, the privacy laws don't allow us to discuss medical issues with anyone not designated by the patient. You must not be on his list."

Betty huffed. "Trust me, Clarence wouldn't mind if we knew about him."

The nurse pulled her hand away from Betty. "Sorry, I can't say."

"What if we promise we won't tell where we heard about his condition?"

The lifting of her eyebrows and her shrug told the sisters that the nurse wouldn't reveal any more information. "Can I get you anything?" she repeated.

"I need a straight answer, but since you won't give it to me, no, we don't need anything."

The nurse smiled. "Your breakfast should be here soon. Maybe that will make you feel better." She breezed out the door.

Betty kicked at the covers on the bed. "I don't like this, Leona! Clarence is our best friend. We ought to go sit by his bed until Tom gets here."

"I know, but there's not much we can do." Leona clasped Betty's hand. "They won't tell us anything. The doctor just says he needs our prayers. Let's say a prayer, shall we?"

Betty snorted. "Pray while you go around to every room in this place and find him! Where's my cane?"

"I don't want to leave you! When Diane comes to sit with you, I'll go looking. She should be here soon."

Betty sat up straight in bed and took the oxygen away from her face. "Forget Diane. If you're not going now, then I will! Get me my cane!"

Leona restrained her and pushed her back onto her pillow. "Okay, I'll go!" Leona smoothed the tubes down, put the oxygen tubes back where they belonged, and looked to see that Betty wasn't bleeding anywhere. "You are so stubborn. Always want to get your own way."

Betty lay there with a gotcha look on her face. "That's what older sisters do. Tell the younger ones what to do. Now don't be too long. I need to know how my honey's doing. And comb your hair before you leave. You look—" She skewed her face with her opinion.

Leona opened her mouth to ask for more details but thought better of it. She found a small comb in her purse in response to Betty's reaction. After checking herself in the mirror, she left to go find Clarence.

Leona found Tom in the ICU waiting room talking with the doctor. Tom looked up and waved for her to join them. She sat down next to him, took his hand, and squeezed it.

"Leona, the doctor is telling me that Dad's pretty bad." Tom looked at the doctor and told him to continue.

"Clarence suffered three wounds. A bullet creased his head but there's no sign of brain swelling. A mild concussion is all he suffered. A bullet went through his upper chest and lodged against his shoulder blade. We removed the bullet and glued the bone together. That should heal and with physical therapy, be able to regain good use of that arm. What concerns us most is the bullet wound in his right chest. It passed through his lung and went out the back. That is our biggest concern. We put a tube in and got the lung reinflated. We'll watch him closely for any sign of pneumonia. He also has cuts and puncture wounds from the shattering glass and bruises from falling. We worry about blood clots and infection developing which means we'll keep him here for a while. He is badly hurt, but barring complications, should recover in time."

Tears streaming down her face, Leona's hand moved to her mouth to stop a sob from exiting. She checked her sleeves for tissues but found none. Tom pulled out his handkerchief and handed it to her.

The doctor took off his glasses and stared at Leona. "Are you one of the ladies who was there when the shooting occurred?" He waved his glasses toward her bloodied slacks.

Leona nodded. "I was in the bedroom. I heard the noise and rushed out to find—find—" She buried her face in the moist handkerchief. The bloody scene would never leave her mind.

"Have you been checked out?"

"No." She wiped her nose and took a deep breath to control her weeping. "I'm okay. Not a scratch."

With a tone that laid bare why he became a doctor, he said, "You should get a doctor to check you over. The trauma might have affected you more than you know." His hand covered hers and she felt his caring and concern. "I could make you an appointment with a counselor."

"Thanks, Doctor. I'll do that in the next few days." She looked at Tom, then back at the doctor.

The doctor looked at his tablet again. "In addition to his wounds, Mr. Brown may have suffered a mild heart attack. To find how much damage may have been caused, we need to do cardiac catheterization. I feel he's strong enough to withstand it. It's something that needs to be done as soon as possible so we can see if he needs stents, but first, we need your permission to do the procedure."

Tom looked at Leona.

He didn't need her concurrence, but she gave it anyway. Maybe he needed her confirmation that he was doing the right thing.

"Sure, Doc, do whatever you think best."

The doctor spent a moment typing on his tablet before rising to leave. "The paperwork is started, and things are set up. A nurse will be back shortly with papers to sign. We'll schedule the procedure for later this morning." He cracked a small smile and left in a rush.

Tom exhaled a big sigh and ran his hands through his thinning, brown hair. He needed a shave, but Leona doubted he'd get one very soon. She put her arms around his faded sweatshirt covered shoulders and gave him a hug. She'd known this man since he was a baby. He'd grown up with her children, and they'd all grown up too fast. Here he was now, making life-and-death decisions about his elderly father.

"What happened, Leona," Tom said through his hands on his face. "How did Dad get shot at your house?"

Leona took her turn running her hands through her mussed hair. She hadn't showered or fixed her hair since yesterday, before the nightmare started. If she could turn back time, she'd let her mother's necklace and Joe's ring go. She was a fool for chasing them. Neither was worth a person's life. First the girl, now Clarence and Betty. She should have left the investigation to Smythe.

"Leona?" Tom looked impatient.

Her shoulders drooped and her back went limp as shame weighed on her. "We've been looking for the people who robbed our house. Apparently, we stepped on some toes somewhere or scared the thieves. Things got out of hand."

"Dad told me about the robbery, but where were the police? Aren't they investigating it?"

"Well, yes and no. You see, we think the detective is behind all the burglaries in town and we felt—I felt I had to play detective and find the thieves myself." She looked up at him. "The police weren't doing anything to catch them. We had to."

Tom's mouth fell open. "What? You, Betty, and Dad have been doing police work?"

Leona held up her hands. "I know it sounds crazy, but it's not. Plainly, something devious was going on. We felt it was our civic duty to expose police corruption. We had to do it ourselves because there was nowhere else to turn."

Tom turned away and covered his mouth with his hand. He stood and paced around, mumbling to himself.

Leona wrung her hands. "We had no idea it would go this far. I'm so sorry."

A nurse came with a folder full of release forms for Tom to sign. Leona escaped while Tom tended to the duties at hand. She couldn't face his wrath even though she deserved it. Clarence would have to find another chauffeur because she was certain Tom would never allow her to take him anywhere again.

Diane stood up when Leona entered Betty's room. Her frown lines were deep and many as she stared at Leona. Her years of tanning had given her an older-than-her-years look. Her black leggings under a too-big sweatshirt and long pink dyed hair added to her nonconformist attitude.

"What have you done to my mother!" The accusation left no room for answering the question, so Leona remained close to the doorway.

"I didn't do it."

"Did you find Clarence?" Betty asked, peering around her outraged daughter who was standing with her hands on her hips. "Did you find anything out?"

"Yes," she said as she kept her eyes on the human pit bull. Diane had always been this way, even as a young girl. Headstrong and obstinate, she never let go of a wrong done against her. She took after her dad in that respect, the opposite end of the spectrum from her mother. "He's in ICU because he was shot three times and had a mild heart attack. They're still doing tests. He should recover from them all, the doctor said. Tom's here with him."

Diane spun around to face Betty. "That does it! Staying with Aunt Leona is hazardous. You're coming home with me, Mother. I know of a nice independent living facility near me that you'll enjoy. They have lots of fun there, and you'll fit right in. You'll be safe there from whatever thugs you're mixed up with thanks to Aunt Leona. Neither of you should be chasing criminals or whatever. I don't know what either of you was thinking."

"She's not old enough to go—" Leona reached out toward the pit bull with a peaceful gesture.

The pit bull shot her a look that seemed like solar flare from the sun.

Leona drew in her hand and took a step back.

A long, fake glittery fingernail pointed at Leona and stabbed the air in her direction like a lance. "I've already talked to Jennifer. She's on her way to take care of you. I will push her to make you sell your house and go live with her."

231

Leona stopped dead in her tracks, blindsided by the remark. Sell her house? No one could make her do that, not even Jennifer or Brett. Fire flashed through her, but she didn't want to hurt Betty by telling her daughter just what she was thinking.

"Diane, go get me a soda from the machine down the hall." Betty said quietly. When Diane refused to break the stare down with Leona, Betty became more insistent. "You heard me, young lady. I want a soda, and I want it now. Go."

Without breaking the gaze, she replied to her mother, "I'll be right back." She sidled around Leona like she was a leper before leaving the room.

Betty reached out to Leona. "How is Clarence? Will he live?"

Leona was still livid at being challenged by this whippersnapper of a niece. Betty was too young to be put in some kind of home. How dare she even suggest it.

Boiling at the temperature of hot lava, she made her way to Betty's bedside. Betty reached out to take her hand and shook it so hard that Leona's upper arm flapped. "Answer my question! Will he live?"

As if coming out of a trance, Leona tried to focus on Betty's earnest face. The emotion there helped Leona push her anger away. "It sounds like he will be fine if infections don't start. He's cut up like you, but they fixed him." She went on to detail all she'd learned from the doctor, except for the part where they told her to get checked out. She ended with, "They think he'll be fine in time, but he'll be in the hospital for a while."

Betty's hand went to her heart. "Oh, thank you, Lord!" She wiped her eyes with the edge of the sheet. "I was so afraid I'd lost him just when I found out how wonderful he is. Leona, brace yourself. I think I love him."

Finally! A topic not about the shooting or retirement homes. It was refreshing, yet weird to think about. "Seeing you two, it hurt my eyes. You and Clarence? It doesn't seem right. He's like one of our brothers."

Betty chuckled softly. "You act like we were doing something wrong." She let out a puff and an eyeroll. "We're not dead yet, you know. Love can still bloom even at our age." Her face blushed as she looked away.

Her face suddenly hot, Leona stared at her feet, wanting them to take her away from the discomfort. "I know, but it was like seeing my brother and sister—you know—I mean, YUCK!"

"Oh, Leona, that's disgusting! Just because you've been around him since you and Joe met doesn't mean he's like MY brother. I only saw him when we came to visit you, and I only got to know him since I moved in with you." She lay back on her pillow and put her hands on her chest. "I'm surprised at how I feel! During this whole thing with the burglary, I started looking at him in a different light. He's a very kind and caring person, and he's lonely. You know I love you, Leona, and I appreciate how you took me in after Vince died, but you don't need me. As much as I love living with you, I miss having someone to take care of. I need to be needed, and Clarence makes me feel needed. We both know he can't take care of himself."

No doubt about that. Betty was born a caregiver, first with dolls and then through her husband Vince who died from Parkinsons. A relationship with Clarence made sense from that perspective.

Leona sat on the edge of the bed and took her sister's hand. "I don't know what I'd have done without you after Joe died. But I can manage on my own now. Clarence will need lots of help when he gets home. He'll be glad he has you around." The sisters hugged until the pit bull returned with Detective Charlie Walters behind her.

CHAPTER 23

Leona hung up the telephone in the kitchen. Drawing a deep breath as she searched for courage, she went to face her daughter in the living room. "That was the insurance adjuster. He's not too happy with me."

Jennifer's jaw hung limp as she surveyed the room. "Tell him to take a number and get in line. Goodness, Mom, what happened here?"

Jennifer stood in front of her mother, tall and thin like her father. She wore jeans and a stylish shirt that made her look younger than her 45 years. She tapped her foot just like Leona used to do.

I used to be that thin, Leona thought. *That girl better be careful, or she'll end up pleasingly plump like me*. Leona almost laughed out loud.

Jennifer gestured at the plywood that covered the picture window and waved her hand toward the bullet holes in the wall. "Who would want to shoot up your house? What did you do?"

"I didn't do anything." The words repeated the phrase Leona had heard so often during Jennifer's teenage years. "I'm not the one who shot the house up." Tired of reciting the same answers

235

to all her questioners, Leona settled into her recliner and put the footrest up.

"Diane says you dragged her mother and Clarence into the seedy parts of town looking for Dad's ring. She said you'd been asking questions and stirring things up with criminals. Criminals with guns! I don't get it. You and Dad would have had a fit if I hung out with people like that."

The truth made her brain ache. "Our house was robbed. I told you about that."

"Yes, and I thought everything was settled. The insurance paid for the things that were stolen and put your house back together."

"It did, but I wanted your father's wedding ring and your grandmother's necklace back. I intended to pass them on to you and Brett."

"Is that when this whole mess started? While you were chasing a couple pieces of jewelry that neither of us want?"

Leona repeated the spiel she'd told Charlie Walters. "The police didn't seem like they were trying very hard, and I wanted my things back. This police detective—Smythe's his name—kept trying to put me off, but I've found out things about him. I think he's involved in some way with the bandit who robbed our house—a scoundrel named T-Bone—and I think he might be a member of the burglary ring and not really a good cop. I think he tried to cover it up."

"Sounds like you've done all kinds of thinking." Jennifer sat on the sofa so she could see her mother. "Did you tell the other police about your suspicions?"

Leona bobbled her head in response.

Jennifer let out a soft groan. "Is that a yes or a no?"

Leona shifted in her chair, uncomfortable with justifying herself to her daughter. "I reported things to the front desk sergeant, but he didn't take me seriously. In fact, the sergeant defended Smythe. I knew they wouldn't listen to me until I had evidence. I was trying to find some."

"You're not a detective, Mom! Let the police handle it."

Leona slammed her hand down on the arm of her chair. "You're right. I should have. Now I've caused more damage and hurt to people I love. I regret it all. I so desperately wanted your dad's ring back, I couldn't think of anything else."

"Did you ever find proof the detective might be involved?"

"We found three young witnesses that said they saw him associating with felons." Leona drew in a quick breath. "The boys! I forgot about the boys!" She jumped out of her chair. "I've got to find out if the boys are okay. I must call Tristan and see if he knows anything. Then I need to call Molly because she's worried about them too." Leona hurried to the kitchen and dialed Tristan's number.

"Who are you calling, Mom?" Jennifer stood behind Leona.

"My lawyer. He knows where the boys are. He can go check on them."

"What boys are you talking about? Does Mr. Lanyard know them?" Jennifer looked confused and worried.

Amber's voice came over the phone, and Leona asked to speak to Tristan. While she waited, she explained to Jennifer. "Ernie

Lanyard ran off with his secretary so a young lawyer, Tristan Wilcox, took over his practice. He's been working with me on—Hello, Tristan? This is Leona. Hey, I need you to do me a favor. Could you go check on my boys? Please? And get back to me as soon as you can. I'm worried about them."

After Leona hung up, she finished telling Jennifer about her boys.

Jennifer cocked her head and frowned. "I can't figure out what you're talking about. You have no boys other than Brett. Did you adopt some without telling me, or has your mind gone soft?"

"Of course not. It's all very tangled and convoluted, but I'll explain it more later. I need to run to the police station and see what Tristan finds out." She went into her bedroom and brushed her hair and put on makeup. After checking on Prissy, who hadn't left Betty's bedroom since the shooting, she returned to the living room.

Jennifer had Leona's purse and was rummaging through it.

"What are you doing?" Leona made a grab for the purse, but Jennifer pulled it back out of her reach.

"You worry me, Mom. You might be losing your mind. I'm taking your car keys, so you don't run off and get into trouble again. I'll give them back later."

Leona lunged at her purse again, but Jennifer sidestepped and held the purse behind her. Leona growled deep in her throat like Prissy sometimes did at her. Another attempt for her purse fell short as well.

This was getting her nowhere but mad. "I'm not nuts, Jennifer. I'm in a hurry. Three little boys need my help, and I won't let them down." She moved toward Jennifer trying to reach her purse.

Jennifer moved away and held the purse out of Leona's reach. "Who are these boys? What are their names?"

"Doran, Jaden, and Tiger. Sweet kids. Miracle kids considering where they are growing up. Their mother is a drug addict, you see—"

Jennifer made a face. "Maybe I need to do my own investigation." She rubbed her forehead as she took a step back. "I might as well tell you that Brett and I think you need to move closer to one of us so we can be there for you if you have problems. This house is too much for you, especially if Diane takes Aunt Betty with her."

"Diane wants to put Betty in an old-folks home." Leona clenched and unclenched her fists. "She's too young for that. And I'm perfectly fine here in my own home. Your father and I bought this for our old age. He won't be here, but I'll stay until they haul me away."

Jennifer's expression softened a little. "Mom, we weren't talking about putting you in a 'home' but a place of your own. We'd be nearby to help if something happened, or you got sick."

Jennifer's pleading eyes infuriated Leona. Her children wanted to take her home away from her and move her to a strange place. All her friends were here. No, she would never do it! She stomped her foot so hard it ached. "No, I won't go. You can't make me!" Why did those words sound so familiar with that face so near?

"We'll talk about it later." Jennifer lifted Leona's keys to her minivan out of her purse and rung them like a bell. "In the meantime, I'm running to the market to get some food." She stuck the keys in her pocket and tossed the purse back to Leona. She turned and went out the garage door. The garage door was raised, and her minivan's motor started.

Leona paced all over the house, seething with rage. Jennifer was holding her hostage in her own home. How dare she! She slammed a towel on the bathroom countertop and stared at herself in the mirror. The veins on her neck were throbbing with her angry heartbeat. She was startled by the sight. She needed to calm down before she had a stroke. If she did, her kids would stash her away in a home somewhere faster than Amazon's overnight delivery.

Going to her recliner in the living room, she plopped down like a cow too tired to go any farther. She rubbed her temples and quoted a Bible verse: *Overcome evil with good*. She felt a little release of tension. *Overcome evil with good*. It helped. She kept repeating the verse, trying to release the pent-up stress.

The phone rang, startling her and jolting her out of her meditation. She held onto her chest to calm her pounding heart and tried to catch her breath before answering. "Hello?" She was still out of breath.

"Leona? Is that you? Were you running?" Tristan's voice sounded genuinely worried.

"Yes, I was. I ran a mile. What's going on?"

"I thought you'd like to know that the boys are being moved to another facility."

"What? Another facility? Why? Who's doing this?"

"Smythe."

Leona's heart started racing again. "No! He can't do that!"

"He filed papers that the boys are troublemakers, and they are being sent to Hughes County."

"He's trying to keep them away from me because he knows that they know me, and they'll tell me the truth. You've got to stop him!"

"The other day, I talked to Charlie Walters who started investigating Smythe's finances. I just talked to him, and he said things looked suspicious. They haven't completed their investigation yet so it's too early to draw any conclusions, but you may be right about him being connected with the burglary ring. If the boys can put the finger on him, they may be in danger."

"When are they being moved?"

"Any time now, if he hasn't already."

"Tristan, you go talk to Charlie or a judge and get him to stop the transfer. I'm on my way down there to stop him if I can. I'll lay down behind his car if I must. We have to save the boys!"

"Let me handle this, Leona— "

"No time to talk. See you downtown!"

Leona hung up the phone and dashed into the kitchen where her purse still sat on the table. Grabbing it, she hurried to Joe's workbench in the garage. She dumped a coffee can of nuts, bolts, and various other metal items on the workbench and pawed through the pile. Pushing the contents around she found what she was looking for. The spare key to the Eldorado.

Once inside the car, she rummaged through her purse to find her cell phone. Her hands shook as she punched the buttons to find her calling list. Her fingers seemed determined to hit the wrong buttons. She massaged her hands and uttered, "Heaven help me!" A moment later, she found the right number. She punched it and hoped he was home. He was. "George, I have a job for our coffee group."

CHAPTER 24

After sitting unused for so long, Leona wasn't sure the Eldorado would even start. She cranked it for several minutes, and at last it roared to life. Driving the ancient car was like maneuvering a tank. Its steering wheel was thinner and slicker than what she was used to. It only had a lap belt, leaving her feeling unprotected without the shoulder strap. Nevertheless, the behemoth car backed out of the garage and transported her down the street.

Leona pulled around to the side of the police station and parked the gunboat of a car. She slid across the bench seat to get out and hurried toward the back of the police station where she knew the main jail was located. When she rounded the corner of the building, she saw Smythe pushing the boys into the back of his car.

"Smythe!" Leona yelled. "You leave those boys alone!" She started running toward him.

Smythe jerked around, his mouth agape. A snarl quickly formed there as he pushed Tiger inside the car.

"Help us, Miz Leona!" Jaden cried out. Smythe pushed his head down and forced him into the backseat with his brothers before slamming the door shut.

"Get out of here, you old biddy!" Smythe growled at her. "I'm tired of your ugly face!" He opened his car door and got in. The engine roared to life as Leona ran up beside the car.

"Stop!" As the car began to move, she pounded on the windows and cried out louder, "Help, police!" She tried to open the door. "Citizen's arrest!"

The car sped up, twirling her as it left her behind. She stumbled backward into another police car where she steadied herself. Falling and breaking a hip wouldn't help the rescue effort. Regaining her equilibrium, she weaved a crooked path back to the Eldorado, her arms splayed out like a balancing pole of an acrobat as she trotted. She got into the giant car and found her cell phone. Thankful for the redial button, she quickly called George. "He's in a black Charger! That's what it said on the trunk anyway. He's headed toward the east side of town. Don't let him get past the city limits!"

George didn't respond at first. "A black Charger? That doesn't give me a lot of help in finding it."

"That's all I know!" she yelled into the phone. "It's a black car with three scared boys in the backseat. Watch for it. Don't let it leave town!" She threw the phone on the bench seat beside her, then started her car. She threw it into gear and pushed the accelerator to the floor. The old, but still powerful motor pressed her back in the seat. The tires squealed in protest at the sharp turn out of the parking lot in pursuit of Smythe. Control of the car almost slipped away as the wheel slid through her palms, but with a mighty grip, she regained it.

She soon caught up with Smythe on Main Street, heading out of town. He wasn't speeding in the 30-mile-per-hour zone. Doing so would have brought a patrol car chasing him. He probably wanted to slip out of town quietly without answering questions. Disguised in her Eldorado, she sneaked up on him in pursuit. If she could get in front of him, maybe she could slow him down until George got there to block him in. He'd have no choice but to stop at that point.

Pulling out from behind him, she eased the Eldorado into the other lane. The light ahead turned yellow and she pulled up beside him. He glanced over to see who was there. His eyes widened in surprise when he saw Leona shaking her fist at him and motioning for him to pull over. He quickly turned right, leaving Leona driving along Main Street.

She sped up and pulled into the other lane before sliding the Eldorado around the next corner. The black Charger went past the intersection ahead. She floored the accelerator to reach the intersection quickly. The stop sign made her brake long enough to see that no one else was coming. The Eldorado leaned heavily on two wheels to make the corner onto Adams Street. With a whomp, it settled back down on all four tires before speeding down the street again, sending a bolt of panic through her. Her insurance might get cancelled if she wrecked her car after they replaced her living room twice.

The black Charger was nowhere in sight. Heading down Adams Street, she caught a glimpse of taillights on a black car on her left as she went through an intersection. Smythe was going back to Main Street.

Leona turned the Eldorado gunboat at the next corner and headed back toward Main. Taking a quick look to see if traffic was coming, she didn't stop as she turned. The black car was a block ahead of her and nearing the edge of town. She pushed the Eldorado until it came up behind the black Charger. A car in the lane beside him blocked her way. Still in no hurry, the two kept the same speed for a block. Smythe had probably called for backup, but she didn't care. Bring on the police. She'd sic them on him.

Her plan wasn't working. She pulled into a Dollar Store parking lot and called George. "He's headed north on Main Street, just past Sixth."

George chuckled as he said, "You were easy to spot with the way you're driving. We've got him. Don't worry. He won't get far."

Pulling back into traffic, Leona watched Smythe as he moved closer to the edge of town. Suddenly, he took a turn back toward Adams Street. When she got to the same corner, she saw him turn right like he was returning to the police station. She followed him a block behind until he turned back toward Main Street.

When she got there, Leona could see a red Chevy pickup and a white Cadillac Escalade slowly driving side by side on Main. It was George's truck and Nick's Escalade! They had forced Smythe to turn back toward Adams Street. Leona turned the corner and headed toward Adams as well.

A police car pulled up behind Leona without its lights on. She glanced at her speedometer. They couldn't stop her for speeding.

She was only going 25 miles per hour. Walters must have sent them after Smythe. Turning on her blinker, she turned on Adams after a complete stop at the stop sign. Up ahead, the black Charger was moving slowly, allowing her to catch up. She followed at a safe distance and stayed in her lane, giving no reason for the police to pull her over.

In the rearview mirror, Leona saw George's Chevy truck behind the police car, but Nick's Escalade was nowhere to be seen. The caravan continued until Smythe turned back toward Main. Leona and the police car turned on their blinkers and followed him.

The edge of town was only two blocks away. Smythe was almost out of her reach. Then what? She couldn't let him out on the open highway. The city policeman behind her would have no jurisdiction after he crossed the city limits. Smythe would take off, and she would never see the boys again!

Back on Main Street, the line of cars slowed almost to a crawl. Leona craned her neck to look around the black Charger. Easing her car closer to the yellow line, she could see cars driving very slowly, impeding traffic. Although she couldn't be sure, a truck straddled the white line, blocking both lanes. And the vehicle looked a lot like Nick's Escalade.

Leona laughed out loud. Her friends had come to the rescue! They were keeping Smythe in town until Tristan got matters settled at the courthouse.

She watched Smythe veer down a small side street. Leona and the police car followed him around the corner. Smythe's brake lights came on and he stopped in the middle of the street. Leona saw

George's red truck across the street with boxes strewn all the way across the road like they had fallen off his truck. He had his back turned to Smythe's car, but she could tell he was talking on his phone.

Before Leona could decide what to do, Smythe's tried to go around the back of the truck right before the Escalade turned down the street facing the Charger.

Seeing the black car's backup lights come on, Leona parked her giant car crossways in the street. They'd done it! Smythe was hemmed in! They had him now!

The lights on the police car flashed on as she pulled into position. At last! She might get a ticket for blocking the road, but the ticketing process would give Tristan more time to get things arranged with the court. The boys would be safe again. Maybe Charlie Walters would complete his investigation of Smythe's finances and have enough to charge him with whatever he found to be wrong.

Things were looking up. A smile came across her face, and she breathed a sigh of relief.

The policemen jumped out of their cars and stayed behind the doors with guns drawn. "Get out of the vehicle! Keep your hands where we can see them."

Leona looked at Smythe's car to see if he was going to comply with the instructions. No movement. He sat as still as a statue.

When he didn't move, she was puzzled. There was no movement in the backseat either. The boys must be huddled on the floor of the car.

Leona heard the policeman yell again. "You! In the car! Get out of your vehicle! Keep your hands in sight!"

Smythe remained frozen in place in his car.

Leona wanted to go over there and pull the man out. Shame on him for not complying with police orders!

The door of Leona's car was flung open, and a policeman was there with his gun pointed at her. "Get out! Keep your hands where I can see them!"

Leona let out a squeal of fright. "ME?" She waved frantically at Smythe's car. "I'm not the criminal! He is!"

"GET OUT OF THE CAR!" The policeman stared down his arm, across his pistol, and into Leona's eyes. "Now."

Leona recognized Don Janus, but she'd never seen him with such determination in his eyes. She put her hands up and stepped gingerly out of the car. Don swung her around so she faced the car, but the motion made her dizzy. She staggered and started to fall. He reached out and steadied her so that she kept her balance.

The radio on his collar buzzed, blending in with the buzzing in her head. She couldn't make out what the message said, but she understood when Don told her, "Wait here." He left her hanging on to the car door as he moved around the Eldorado with his gun drawn and moved toward Smythe's car. Olivia Torrez came from behind Leona to join him.

"Smythe, get out of the car, sir!" Don stood with his gun held in both hands pointed at the driver's seat. Leona could see Smythe staring straight ahead, gripping the steering wheel. "Sir, get out and keep your hands where I can see them."

Smythe drooped his head. He pulled out a gun and held it against his head.

"Don't do it, Smythe! Don't do it!" Olivia yelled through the window.

Seeing the gun, Leona rushed around her car and came up behind the cops. "Not in front of the boys! Please! Not in front of the boys!" Her impassioned plea rang through the air around them all. "They've seen too many bad things in their short lives. Don't make it one more."

Time stood still as everyone watched the man with the gun to his head. With sloth-like speed, the gun began to move down. When it was no longer visible, breath came back to Leona. Olivia opened Smythe's door and took the gun out of his hand. Don opened the back door, and the three boys came spilling out. They ran to Leona, wrapping themselves around her while she moved them away from the Charger.

CHAPTER 25

Leona stood on the front porch of her home while she waved good-bye to Jennifer. Once the car was out of sight, Leona let out a yell of freedom and went inside.

"You seem happy." Betty sat on the sofa crocheting. Daylight streamed through the new picture window behind her. Prissy, sitting next to her, gave Leona her usual frown. She hadn't let Betty get too far away since she'd been home from the hospital.

"I love my daughter, but she's too bossy for me to enjoy her for long." Leona sat in her recliner and picked up the newspaper, pulling up the footrest. She thought about turning on her new 65-inch flat screen TV but thought better of it. She took a sip of coffee before settling in to read. "There's an article about Smythe on the front page of the paper today."

"Yes, I know. I read it. I feel sorry for him."

Leona put the paper down. "Because of him, you nearly got killed, not to mention Clarence and his heart attack."

Betty shook her head without looking up from her crocheting. "He got himself into a bad situation and was trapped. He helped the burglary ring so he could pay for his wife's cancer medicine. He couldn't afford it otherwise. He did it for love, not personal gain."

"Why didn't he stop after his wife died?"

"T-Bone wouldn't let him. He threatened to expose him, kill him, and whatever other unpleasant things he could think of. Smythe had no choice but to go along."

"No one forced him to kidnap the boys! He was taking them to who knows where so they'd be out of the picture."

"The article says T-Bone threatened them too. Smythe was moving them to keep them safe from his band of miscreants."

Leona grumbled as she unfolded the paper. "Doesn't matter. He doesn't deserve any sympathy. Whatever happens to him, he brought it on himself. He's a crooked cop and should pay for it." She folded the paper so she could read every word. Her heart softened a little when she turned to the inside page for the continuation of the story.

When she finished the article, Leona felt differently. "Okay, so maybe he had a good reason for acting the way he did. He could be considered a victim of the medical system and love for his wife. He made a bad decision and ended his career. That doesn't mean I have to like him."

"No, it doesn't, but don't be bitter." She put down her project and invited Prissy into her lap. "Everything turned out in the end. T-Bone admitted he killed his girlfriend and ordering the drive-by shooting. He and his gang are in jail for a long time. Molly will be glad to have him out of her neighborhood."

That thought hadn't occurred to her. Molly's neighborhood would be much safer. She could go visit more often without worrying about being attacked by the ruffians across the street.

"Everything is as you wanted it. Smythe is off the police force." Betty stroked Prissy who purred like a new engine. "Molly's neighborhood is safer. The boys are back home with their mother." She stopped and frowned slightly. "Well, maybe not everything."

Betty's phone rang. Prissy's purring ceased as she reached into her pocket to get it.

Leona went to get the coffee pot to refill both their cups. A shout of delight drew her back into the living room.

Betty's smile on her face lit up the room. "That was Tom. Clarence is coming home tomorrow!"

Leona smiled back at her. "That's wonderful news!"

"It's the best news of all. We can provide meals and clean the house for him. I can read to him and...oh, and he might need help changing bandages." She counted off each item on her fingers.

Leona returned to the kitchen to let Betty make her list of chores in private. Helping a neighbor was important, but she drew the line at changing stinky, dirty bandages. Her strong gag reflex was one reason she hadn't become a nurse.

She cut the corner off a pan of brownies and popped the piece in her mouth. Its rich flavor and sweetness filled her whole spirit with serenity, and she closed her eyes. Chocolate! Her personal nirvana drug.

"Leona!" Betty broke the chocolate spell. "He's coming home!" She giggled like a schoolgirl. "He's coming home!" She sang as she danced into the kitchen with Prissy at her feet trying to avoid getting stepped on.

Leona leaned against the cabinet. "You're really in love with him, aren't you."

Betty stopped and stared at her sister, then started dancing again. "I am!" She broke out in a crazy love-stricken laugh that frightened Leona a little.

"Has he proposed?"

Betty rubbed her finger along the countertop. "No, not exactly. But I expect he will. He's a lonely man, you know."

"Yes, you told me." Betty needed someone as badly as Clarence did. She'd have to get used to seeing them loving on each other, but it still made her insides cringe a little.

"I guess life will change for all of us."

Betty was quiet for a moment. Her face slowly transformed into a worried look. "That will be hard on you. You'll be all alone for the first time in your life. Do you want me to leave Prissy with you? She'd keep you company."

"Thanks, but no." A cat couldn't replace having Joe around. The house would seem very empty with only her in it, but the idea was exhilarating. She could control everything without interference. Plus, without Prissy around, her furniture and carpet would be free of cat hair.

Betty broke into her thoughts. "We could all live together in one house. You know. Clarence could sell his house and you sell yours.

We could buy a big fancy house with a mother-in-law apartment only it would be a sister-in-law apartment. It would be cheaper for all of us that way."

The idea wasn't crazy but had little in it for Leona. "Who would clean it?" She laughed. "I just fought off Jennifer who wanted me to sell my house. I'm not leaving. I love my house, and I'm staying here."

"Here we are!" Betty let out an excited yell as the trio pulled into Clarence's driveway. Tom pulled his sports car up to the curb. Leona got Clarence's new walker out of the back of the minivan and brought it around. Betty and Tom helped Clarence out of the minivan while Leona stood away from the fussing and let the other two guide and encourage Clarence toward his front door.

George and Irene stood on the porch, welcoming the group home and holding the front door open as Clarence made his way through. The living room was tidied and clean. The piles of magazines were still there but were neatly stacked and dusted. The kitchen sparkled. Casseroles with written heating instructions filled the refrigerator. The house hadn't been this organized since Barbara died.

Leona stood on the front step and wondered whether she should go inside. During one of her and Betty's many visits to the hospital, Tom had spoken angry words to her about endangering

255

his father's life. All she could do in response was apologize. When Tom finished his well-rehearsed tirade against her, he seemed to feel better. They parted on amiable terms, but their relationship had changed.

She got Clarence's bag and accoutrements from the hospital out of the minivan and took them into the house. Clarence was sitting in his recliner while Betty flittered around him, making sure he had his remotes and anything else within reach. Leona set the bags down, then took his big-lidded cup into the kitchen to get him some water.

"Thank you for everything, Leona, George, and Irene," Clarence said from his chair. "God bless you all. You did a lot of work to get this place to look this good. I guess it was a mess."

"Yes, it was," Irene offered before George came up behind her and nudged her.

George waved his arm toward everyone. "It was a group effort. "Don't be surprised if Carly gives you one of her talks about keeping your house clean. Since you seem well taken care of, we'll go and leave you to get settled." They bid all good-bye and left.

Tom came out of the back bedroom and got the bags. "Thanks for bringing him home, Leona. I think he's more comfortable in your minivan than in my sports car."

"You're welcome. I'm always happy to give him rides." She turned to go. "How long will you be here?"

Tom shrugged. "Through the end of the week, then I need to get back to work."

"If I don't see you again, have a safe trip home. Clarence, if you need anything, you've got my number."

"I'll be home in a bit." Betty stood behind the recliner with her hands on Clarence's shoulders.

As Leona turned to leave, Clarence yelled out, "Wait!" He struggled to get out of his chair. "I want you to be here for this!"

Tom pushed his father back into the recliner. "Dad, what do you need? Just tell me what you want, and I'll get it for you."

Clarence let out an exasperated groan. "It's not something you can help me with." He held his hand out toward Betty. "Come here, sweetheart," he said in a singsong voice. "I wanted to get down on one knee to say this, but Sonny boy here won't let me out of this chair."

Eyebrows couldn't have gone any higher nor mouths opened any further as they watched Clarence take Betty's hand. "I love you, Betty Drummond, and I'm asking you to be my wife. Let's spend the rest of our golden years together. What do you say?"

Betty giggled. "You don't need to be on one knee to say that. I love you too, Clarence Brown, and would love to be your bride." She leaned down, and they kissed. On the lips. Not just once, but three times.

Tom frowned. "My dad?"

Leona recoiled. "My stars!"

Clarence smiled. "My sweetheart."

Betty beamed. "My darling."

Leona pulled her minivan into her garage. The world felt different. She hated change. That's why she and Joe had lived in the same house for forty-eight years, in the same town they'd both been born and raised in. When Betty first arrived, she'd gone through a period of awkwardness and adjustment. Watching Clarence propose to her made her realize that now she didn't want her to leave.

Opening the door to the house, Prissy came up to greet whoever stepped inside. She took one look and went back to Betty's bedroom.

Only the humming of the refrigerator filled the silence. Leona's shoes clacked on the kitchen floor, echoing through the empty house. Her life was that way, especially without Joe. Empty. Lonely.

She didn't know what to do with herself but would find purpose somewhere. This being-alone thing would require more modifications than she'd expected. She went to the bedroom and sat on the bed. Opening the nightstand drawer, she pulled out the dark silver pistol she'd purchased after her visit to the pawnshop. It felt light in her hands. She marveled at how pretty it looked. It was empty and needed ammo. She took it to the kitchen and held it in the sink as she turned the faucet on. The flowerpots around the house needed watering.

She danced around the house, acting foolishly and shooting her houseplants with her new toy. She laughed out loud. The pawnshop owner told her to get a gun and she had: a water gun. It looked like the real thing, except for the orange tip where the water came out. The toy seemed enough. She only wanted to scare an intruder, not make the decision whether to shoot someone or not.

She aimed at her zeezee plant in the corner of the living room. Taking careful aim, she pulled the trigger. The stream from the gun reached out maybe four feet, almost reaching the plant. She took a step closer and tried again, this time hitting her target.

Damp lines on the carpet showed her improving aim. As she emptied her gun on her English ivy plant, she decided that maybe being alone wasn't so bad after all. In fact, it might be fun. She let out a laugh at herself.

Her phone rang, drawing her away from her childish play of watering her house plants. She got it on the third ring. "Hello?"

"Leona? This is Charlie Walters. I have a proposition for you."

CHAPTER 26

Life changed even more for Leona with that phone call, but this change she didn't mind. The boys' mother had been found unresponsive in the backyard and was sent to a detox unit. Charlie Walters pulled strings and arranged for the boys to live with her until something more permanent could be arranged. He gave her three days to get her house ready for Child Protective Services' approval.

Her office was quickly packed up and moved to the closet. She found bunkbeds at a thrift store, along with clothes for the boys to wear. A few toys and stuffed animals were added for good measure.

Betty baked a freezer full of cookies in those three days. With her duties of taking care of Clarence, she spent a lot of time running back and forth across the street. Prissy went with her. If she was going to live there, she may as well get Prissy used to her new home.

Leona picked the boys up from their foster family on a Tuesday. Their first stop was at McDonald's for happy meals all round. They acted like being with Leona and having special treats was almost more than their little hearts could contain. More than once, she had to tell them to use their indoor voices and manners.

A stop to see Molly was less stressful now that T-Bone was gone. The boys brought shakes for Zilo and Kendra and told them about how scared they were when the policemen took them. Leona had to set the record straight. Smythe truly was taking them somewhere so that T-Bone couldn't hurt them. It turned out he had a heart after all.

Later that night, the boys were almost too excited to go to bed. Leona had Doran read books to the little boys as she tried to keep them calm. She sat on the edge of the bed but had to leave the big ceiling light on to read.

"This will never do," Leona looked up at the ceiling light. "You need a lamp and a nightstand for bedtime reading, Doran. That way you won't have to get out of bed to turn out the light. We'll look for one for you tomorrow."

Tiger looked puzzled. "What's a nightstand?"

"You know, it's that small piece of furniture beside my bed. Haven't you looked in my room?"

"You mean that little table with the lamp on it?"

Leona laughed. "Yes, that small dresser with the lamp and the alarm clock."

Jaden's eyebrows knitted together. "You got two of them. Do you need them both?"

Leona stopped. The answer was so obvious. "You're right. I only need one. Let's go get that extra one for you to use."

The boys sprang out of bed and raced into her room with her close behind. She unplugged Joe's lamp and alarm clock and set them on the floor. The boys pulled the heavy nightstand away from the wall. As they did so, they heard a light clink. They tilted the stand to one side while Tiger looked under it. He got up holding a gold ring in his hand. Joe's ring!

Leona gasped and grabbed it from the boy. She cradled it as a sob burst from her lips. The boys looked scared as the tears flowed down her face.

"You found it!" She wiped her wet cheeks. "You found it! It must have fallen under there during the burglary and was hidden from the thieves." She held it against her heart. She closed her eyes and envisioned a much-loved face. "My Joe is back."

Opening her eyes again, she saw the frightened faces of the boys staring at her. She wiped her tears away and told them, "I'm crying because I'm so happy. This is the ring I was looking for when—when I found you." She gathered them all in a hug before helping them move the nightstand to their room.

The boys took the drawers out and between Doran and Jaden, they wrestled the nightstand down the hall to their room and alongside their beds. Tiger brought the alarm clock and Leona carried in the lamp. She plugged everything in and set the right time on the clock as the older boys brought the drawers.

"There. Now you can set the alarm and get yourselves up for school if you're still here then." She helped them into their beds.

Tiger's eyes almost overran with tears. "Can't we stay with you forever?"

Leona pulled him into her lap. "I hope to be in your lives forever, but people are building a new house for Molly, and she'll be your foster mother. But don't worry. I'm not going anywhere."

His tears dried except for one that slid down his cheek.

She hugged him tighter. "Molly wants you to live with her. She loves you as much as I do. I'll be your grandma, and you won't be able to keep me away."

"She can't have us here, Tiger," Doran said. "She's too old to keep us."

Ouch! That stung, but she knew he only meant it in a kind way. "Um, that's not it. I have to help take care of Betty and Clarence, and they're a handful. But don't worry, I'll love you forever."

Tiger wiped his eyes with the sleeve of his pajamas and seemed happy with her answer.

"Who does that ring belong to? Why did you want it so bad?" Jaden asked as she tucked the boys in.

Leona smiled to herself. "It belonged to my husband. He wore it for more than 40 years while we were married."

"What happened to your husband?"

"He died of a heart attack two and a half years ago." Her voice faded away as the memory threatened to take her out of the present.

"Do you think he'd have liked us? Would he have let us stay here with you?"

Leona stared at three pairs of questioning eyes. If he'd been here, she'd never have met the boys who filled her heart so full.

"Granny Leona? You okay?" Doran took his arm out from under the covers and patted her hand. "Are those happy tears?"

She shook herself out of her runaway thoughts and wiped her eyes. "If he were still alive, I wouldn't have gone looking for his ring. T-Bone would still be robbing houses, and I'd have never met Molly, the sweetest woman I've ever met. I'd have never met you either."

Doran's brow furrowed as he thought. "I'm not happy your Joe died, but I'm glad he's not here." His eyes brimmed with tears as he looked at her. She pulled him into an embrace.

Jaden looked very sober. "I'm glad we met you too. Good thing your house got robbed."

Tiger kicked his feet and Leona had to tuck him in again. "Yeah, I'm glad you got robbed too. I like it here!"

She tucked the covers around the boys. "Remember, you're only here until Molly's new house is ready. Then you'll live with her so you can see your mom and uncle from time to time. But don't worry, you can visit me anytime. Just call so I can give you a ride over. No more walking!" She tickled the boys, and their laughter rang through the house. "Now get some sleep. You've had a big day."

Doran, ever the thoughtful thinker, piped in, "Should we tell that policeman thank you for having T-Bone rob your house?"

Leona thought. That's what started it, the house burglary. It had changed her life in more ways than she thought possible. And it had changed Smythe's life too. Because of Leona's persistence, he'd been investigated and arrested that day when he was taking the boys to another town. He became a witness for the prosecution of T-Bone and his gang, and additional details had come out. He'd planted drugs in Leona's minivan because he knew T-Bone was planning to kill her, and Smythe knew she'd be safer in jail for a night or two. Too bad she vacuumed it out when she washed her van. He truly was moving the boys to safety when he was finally arrested. Those actions and a plea deal got him three years of jail time and 10 years of probation. Since he couldn't be held in the area with the other prisoners, he sat in a cell alone day after day. Ostracized by his former colleagues, he led a lonely life, although Leona heard he was writing a book about his experiences. It would be good therapy for him.

"Maybe we can write him a letter."

"But I can't write," Tiger said.

Jaden answered before Leona could. "Don't worry. You can draw the pictures."

Leona told the boys goodnight and went to her room. She placed Joe's ring on his pillow. It seemed a silly place to keep something so dear. No wonder she'd lost it. Snatching it, she went to the kitchen and got an envelope from the drawer. Back in her room, she sealed the ring inside the envelope and buried it in the top drawer of her bureau. Never again would she let it or any other possession control her. Memories and people still alive were enough to fuel her soul.

With the ring stored, she opened another drawer and pulled out the water gun she didn't want the boys to know she had. Her flowers needed water before she enjoyed her new larger-than-ever TV.

The End

ACKNOWLEDGEMENTS

This book was inspired by my many adventurous friends who are my age. Back when we were young, we didn't trust anyone over 30. We couldn't imagine ourselves ever being that old, but time passes whether we like it or not. Here we are in our 60s and 70s, living life to its fullest while we can and having a good time doing it.

Also, the many lawyer and crime shows, along with the more recent Murder She Wrote episodes, inspired this book. I love watching them more than the modern shows. The fashions and cars were better back then, and the characters never had blood on them even after hurt or shot. They don't make shows like they used to.

Thanks to my husband for his constant support while I'm writing, marketing, and signing my books. He even bought me noise-cancelling headphones so I could write in peace and quiet. He's the best. Thanks, honey!

And thank you, dear reader, for your time and support. PLEASE leave a review so I know what you thought of this book. It's the best thing you can do for me and any author. If you liked my book, please tell your friends, family, and book clubs.

ABOUT THE AUTHOR

C.S. Kjar is an award-winning author who lives out west where the deer, antelope, and bison play. Most of her books are filled with fun, adventure, and mystery, and some were even finalists in national competitions. Her writing is for ages from eight to eighty or more, fun and light-hearted with touches of humor and wisdom. Her books are a great way to escape from harsh realities into a world where love and hope are the greatest possessions of all.

Her last name is pronounced "care" which she loves. She cares about you having good books to read, and it's what we should all do: care for each other.

All books by C.S. Kjar are listed on her website at cskjar.com.

ALSO BY C.S. KJAR

All of her books can be found on her website at cskjar.com.

Sweet Romance

The Treasure of Adonis

The Christmas Eve Wedding

Finding Love in the Snow

Women's Fiction/Contemporary Fantasy

The Daughters of Time Series:

Book 1: The Secrets of the Clock

Book 2: The Secrets of the Cottage

Book 3: The Secrets of the Storm

Children's Book

The Five Grannies Go to the Ball

Nonfiction

Scraps of Wisdom: All I Needed to Know I Learned in Quilting
Class

www.ingramcontent.com/pod-product-compliance
Lightning Source LLC
Chambersburg PA
CBHW021004260626
47169CB00006B/1943